MY HUMAN PET

OLYMPIA BLACK

Printed in the United States of America

First Printing: March 2020

ISBN-13 : 979-8624213869

ISBN-13 : 979-8507344970

NOTE FROM THE AUTHOR

My books are not for the faint of heart.

I must thank Alma Nilsson for her creative world-building which inspired this story.

Another of Mack's patients says that the aliens have been taking eggs from her since she was sexually mature, and that her reproductive system baffles her gynecologist. Is it baffling enough to write the case up and submit a research paper to The New England Journal of Medicine? Apparently it's not that baffling.

Carl Sagan

The Demon-Haunted World: Science as a Candle in the Dark

ABBREVIATIONS

- IGC: Imperial Galaxy Court
- IC: Instant Communicator
- UC: Universal Credit

CHAPTER 1

nsley

"Shark attack!" I scream as I slap my phone to turn the irritating *Jaws* themed alarm off. *How is it eight in the morning already?* I wonder. I angle my body and let myself slowly fall off the bed with a soft thump.

Now I'm lying on my cold and dirty, wooden floor, half-covered with garments that didn't win the honor of being chosen for 'the perfect outfit' last night.

After a few seconds, I open my eyes, again. A pair of black jeans are looking suspiciously right back at me.

I'm so hungover, I think, and I take the Lord's name in vain.

Then I reminisce about the night before, random images of laughing and drinking dance dizzily through my alcohol-soaked mind making me even more lightheaded and nauseous. I frown. My best friend is moving to a god-forsaken fly-over state today. She met a man online who had only been visiting New York City. I didn't agree with her decision, but when your best friend tells you she is in love, what can you do? You buy her a drink. You buy her several.

Love is madness. All those hormones rushing through your body, making sure you are only thinking with one organ, and it's not your brain. I've never been in love, only lust, but I've seen enough friends affected by love to know it makes you irrational, at best.

I had told my friend, after fifteen cocktails, "We're New Yorkers. We aren't meant to leave, we'll die outside our natural habitat." I was only half-kidding. For me, this is where I'm from and I would never willingly leave. Not that I have a great life. I can barely make rent, but NYC is my hometown.

Back to the jeans staring me down. *"Yes, I'm getting up,"* I tell my discarded clothing, as I slowly rise, the room spinning just a little bit faster every inch I go up. I must do this. I have to get to work. It's Saturday and I don't have the luxury of sleeping in.

It's pathetic that even after a college degree and landing a decent white-collar job, I still have to work weekends just to make ends meet.

I go into the old '80's style light blue bathroom with bad lighting. I take one look at my ratty long blonde hair and start quickly braiding. I do an old-fashioned braid around my head and pull some loose strands out, so it doesn't look like I have time-traveled from early 20th century Bavaria. Then I check out the status of my makeup from last night. I wore lots of black eyeliner and with just a little touch up I'm going to keep what I have on rather than washing my face. I just don't have the energy to wash my makeup off and then reapply with hungover shaky hands. If I don't wear makeup, I won't get any tips, just nerdy men trying to start up conversations while I am trying to politely take orders and make cute Instagram-worthy cappuccinos.

I pee like I've never peed in my life, then go back to my bedroom. I sigh at the mess and catch sight of my naked body in the full-length mirror. I'm 24 years old and do my best to keep fit, *These big nights out don't help my bank account or my health*, I think, as I push and shake on my little bloated tummy from last night's meal and drinks. I forget about my bloated stomach as I pull on some clean hot pink lace underwear, a pair of faded black jeans, and a fashionably worn black t-shirt that shows off my large rose tattoo on my wrist and another organic floral tattoo down my right arm. I like flowers, and I like colorful tattoos on my body. Not everywhere, but tastefully done on my arms and wrists. My parents say I'll regret it when I'm older, but I keep reminding them that I am older now and don't regret it. When I look at my reflection, I decide I don't look too bad given my real physical state. I grab my black bag, sunglasses, and go. I'm proud of myself, I'm not even going to be late.

It takes me an hour to walk to work. I would rather walk than take the subway. I'm a New Yorker after all. The most pleasurable part of my commute on Saturdays is walking through Central Park. It's beautiful and sunny this morning. I'm wearing my sunglasses and listening to my favorite new song on my phone with my headphones, not paying attention to anything at all and then suddenly, I'm falling.

Falling.

Falling.

I'm so frightened.

I worry I'm going to have a heart attack.

Have I fallen in water?

I realize, it's not water, it's a strange cold jelly-like material surrounding every inch of me. Invading even my mouth and nose. I think, *This is the end.* My last thought, *I don't want to be one of those people that suddenly dies for unexplained reasons.*

I DON'T KNOW how much time passed before I open my eyes again. I put my hand on my head, my sunglasses are gone. Everything is gone. Everything but my black bra and hot pink underwear. I'm in a metal cage. There are harsh shadows of the bars all through it. If I wasn't so scared, I might have thought the contrast of the bright white lights and the shadows of the bars made a magnificent pattern and would have wanted to take a picture of it and post it online. But everything is gone, my phone my clothing and my freedom.

I look around, there are three other half-naked women in this shadow candy cane cage with me. The first thing I think, *I've been traf-ficked!* I open my mouth to speak, but I can't. My mouth is so dry. My hands fly to my throat, in vain, as if touching it will make it feel better. I remember the jelly that invaded my mouth and a wave of disgust washes over me.

One of the other women notices that I'm awake and points to a little water jug on the side of the cage. I look back at the woman in disbelief, thinking, *This can't be happening. I'm not the kind of woman who gets trafficked.*

The same woman who pointed out the water is still staring at me, when we make eye contact again, she shrugs as if to say, It-is-what-it-is, and then looks away.

I slowly get to my feet and move towards the gigantic pet-like water jug. I feel like I've been drugged. Nothing seems right. All my senses seem dull. I shake my head, trying to dispel the sluggish feeling, but it doesn't help. I curse our traffickers in my mind, *Bastards, if you are going to drug us at least use the good kinds of drugs.*

I focus on the water jug and move towards it. Surreally, I reach out and touch it. It's made of a strange material, not glass or plastic. It's surprisingly flexible and fluid. It looks like water floating with a silver straw but contained by an unseen force. I hesitate. I'm so thirsty, I need to put my mouth on the large silver straw and suck like a hamster. But I don't want to do it. I look back around the cage to assess who else has put their lips here. I evaluate the three other women, they all appear to be about the same age as I am, and we are all just here in our bras and underwear.

I decide that none of the women look like they have herpes or the measles or anything like that, so it's probably safe to take a sip of water. I put my lips to the cold metal and suck, humiliated. I'm relieved that when I suck, the water tastes fine and almost good. After a few seconds, humiliation is replaced by gratefulness for the cold water.

I sit back down on the cold metal floor, my belly full of cold water, and address the three other women.

"Do any of you know where we are?" I can see that the other

women have been crying as the remnants of their makeup is all over their faces like sad clowns with vertical tear tracts on their cheeks. The sight gives me a sinking feeling in the pit of my stomach.

The woman who pointed out the water bottle to me says, "We are on a UFO. Aliens abducted us. Probably for experiments. No, I'm not kidding, so wipe that stupid smile off your stupid face."

I thought she must be joking. I couldn't help but smile. I wondered if she were on drugs and if she had more to share or perhaps, they had given her the good drugs. I eyed her, wondering if she had some good drugs hidden in her bra, underwear or vagina. I didn't care. If we were trafficked, we might as well be high in the cage, it was better than crying.

"I know," she continues. "I didn't believe it at first either. I thought these other women were on drugs. That is until I saw our captors. Little freaking green men, just like in all those stupid documentaries about people who claim to have been kidnapped by aliens or visited Area 54 or whatever."

I hold up one hand splayed out with all my fingers and I hold up my other hand with only my index finger up to indicate it is Area 51 she means, but she only rolls her eyes at me and continues.

She lifts up her arm and shows me a high-tech bracelet.

"They're going to give you one of these after they do a medical check. Then you'll see. It's all very real. Way too damn real. I only wish I was on just a really bad trip."

I don't know what to say. I don't really believe in aliens. I've seen the documentaries she's talking about and, I guess, I think there must be some kind of other intelligent life in the galaxy, but like most people, I'm under the impression, that aliens, if they are out there, want nothing to do with Earth or humanity for whatever reason. I can imagine a hundred or more reasons why intelligent life in the galaxy would avoid us. Most likely because we are ridiculous. We still have wars, poverty, hunger, and above all, we destroy our only home with garbage because we allow some greedy billionaires to rule over all of us. Not because we don't know better or we are weak, but only because we are stupid and are too lazy to work together. No doubt, aliens think we are idiots for living in our own filth by choice. Despite our technology we are no better than barbarians with cavemen alphas still taking everything from everyone else in their immediate vicinities.

I think, *And I'm unlucky enough to be picked up for experiments by some aliens rather than live on my trashy planet. Great.* I begin to feel sorry for all the chimpanzees that get picked up for medical testing, and a thought occurs to me, "But if they're green and not like us, it can't be for medical testing, right? I mean, we use chimps and primates for testing because they're almost exactly like us. What kind of experiments do you think these green aliens want us for?"

"Maybe they're going to teach us to do tricks like dolphins at Sea World," the same woman says sarcastically. "Or maybe they are going to cut us up for investigation? And put us all back together again like human women Frankensteins?"

"I'll have your boobs," one of the other women says sarcastically and then she points to the other woman, "and your butt."

"Whatever," the first woman says. "I'm just going on information from every documentary I've ever seen and all the people said what the aliens did to them. Medical experiments with little green men. And besides, rats and rabbits and all kinds of other animals are used for all kinds of weird experiments on Earth for shampoo and stuff. Maybe it's fitting, they are going to be testing us for alien makeup."

"Or we could be a favorite food for a gigantic snake or something," the woman in the corner suggests quietly. "My brother had a snake and he would buy mice from the pet store to feed it. What if we are the mice to a dragon? What if those old knight stories are true and dragons used to eat us on Earth until we killed them all?"

"There were never dragons," I say as if it's the most ridiculous thing I've ever heard.

"And I didn't think there were aliens either, but here we are," she replies.

I use my fingernail to dig into my palm to see if I can feel it hurt and if it really bleeds, "I don't even know if this is real," I say it more to myself than the other three women.

"Oh, it's real," says another woman. "You'll feel that keenly when they take you into the medical area. Then, you won't forget how very real all of this is."

I was just about ready to reply with a snarky comment when the door to the outer room opens and sure enough, two little green aliens come into the room.

The aliens are slight and wear no clothing. I can't see any genitals, so I assume that's why they don't wear any clothing.

Their eyes are big, black, and set far apart like a reptile's would be, I can see a section of our cage reflected in their large black eyes as they come closer and I'm so nervous all I can think is, *Objects in the mirror may appear closer than they really are.* I push my fingernail into my palm again to focus my thoughts. I gather my courage which isn't difficult because this is all so strange, it doesn't even feel real. Again I wonder about the drugs. I stand, "Hi. I think there's been a mistake. I'm from New York. I didn't want to leave, ever. Please take me home. I'll give you whatever you want." I lie. Of course, I have nothing to give.

I ignore the snide remarks under the breaths of the other women in the cage as I try to pleadingly look into one of the deep dark eyes of my captors.

One of the green aliens comes over with a small circular device, opens the cage door, and then shocks me. It hurts so much. I can't even scream with pain. Instead of falling to the floor, cold and slimy green hands catch me.

The aliens begin to escort me, by half-dragging me, out of the room.

My heart starts beating faster and faster. I feel like I can't breathe. I wildly look back to the other women, and one of them mouths the words, 'medical exam,' and I try to calm myself. *None of the other women died from this. Neither will I, right? I'm just as healthy as they are. Except for all the blood in my system. Jesus, I mean the alcohol.* I think about the appearances of the other women, *One is totally a hillbilly and probably has meth in her system, and if they kept her, they are definitely keeping me.* I keep reminding myself about her as we enter the cold clinical silver alien medical lab.

There is an insanely bright light in the room. The same blinding white light that all alien abduction survivors always mention. Before I can reflect on it too much, the green aliens suddenly hoist me up onto a freezing, metal bed with a levitation device. Instantly, frigid metal straps tightly appear around my neck, wrists, and ankles. Just when I think things cannot get any worse, the bed begins to move, pulling my arms and legs apart. I scream, but a liquid jelly that tastes of nothing and has no temperature fills up my entire mouth. I begin to worry I'm going to suffocate to death, but I realize that I'm still breathing through my nose. I try not to panic. I can't help my eyes frantically darting around everywhere though and I'm beginning to freak out because all I see is the bright white light.

All I can hear is the soft and off-beat clicking noises of what I suppose is alien machinery and delicate alien medical tools. I focus on staying alive, not freaking out and giving myself a heart attack. I know they are touching me, but I can't feel a thing, not even numbness. It's surreal to be so strangely violated, and I know by instinct I'm being violated.

My mind is racing with all the possible nasty alien things they could be doing to me while I lie here, paralyzed. I imagine these aliens opening me up, exposing my uterus in order to steal some eggs or put a hybrid alien baby in my womb. Everything I've ever seen on those alien abduction shows comes storming back into my thoughts, and I almost pass out from my own imagination about what's happening. My heart is pounding so fast, I'm sweating, and I begin to wonder again if I'm going to die. Die here with these green aliens. Heartbreaking to not even feel a thing, not even die screaming. It seems like the worst way for my short vibrant life to end, to not even mark it with a scream like those in horror films. I know tears are falling from my eyes, but there's nothing I can do. I'm trapped in this silence.

I remind myself of the other women in the shadowy striped cage and my competitiveness finally kicks in. I think, *I'll not be beaten,* and I rally myself to stay alive. Over and over, I keep telling myself, *I'll not be beaten by ugly green aliens.*

After what seems like an eternity, but is probably only an hour, a black futuristic bracelet, like the other women's is slapped on my wrist, and I'm returned to the cage. I'm only shaky from my own terrible thoughts about what must have been done to me under those bright lights. After I'm released, I take stock of my mind and body. Physically, I can't find anything amiss, which makes me question my sanity.

As soon as the green aliens leave the outer room, the other women begin mocking me.

"So, Miss New York, did you really think aliens would care where you were from?"

"It was worth a try. I wasn't going to merely surrender myself like you all," I'm not surprised that it was the one who looked like she did meth chained to a wall who had asked me that question.

The woman, who had pointed out the water jug to me, stands and displays more than a few big nasty bruises on her arms and shoulders, "I'm from St. Paul, it's in Minnesota, if you didn't know and I tried a damn sight more than you to get out of here."

Another woman turns and shows me a long cut down her side, from her breast to her hip, that is only just healing, "I'm from Oklahoma and I tried to run when they opened the door for another women's medical check, and those green guys cut me so deep that I couldn't get much further than the door without collapsing and they only healed me this much, I guess, to keep me tame."

"I was the first one here," the woman against the wall says. "I tried to run the last two times women were put in here with me, that's why they have chained me to the wall." She rattles her strange alien chain made of strange blue lights. "And I'm not from New York either. I'm from the real part of our country. I'm from Kentucky."

"I guess I always thought women from the rest of the country were…." I trail off. I feel a little bit like an ass now, but not enough to care. It pleases me that I was probably right about the meth head from Kentucky.

"Whatever," Hillbilly says looking at the metal wall. "We all made fun of you while you were getting your medical exam and it was the first time we've had a good laugh since we got here."

My cheeks grow warm with anger.

"What are you going to do now? Lecture us?" taunts Hillbilly, "We all tried to escape, you were just the worst at it." She laughs like someone in an insane asylum, "Apparently you thought just by being from New York would be enough to grant you your freedom. It's hilariously stupid, but none of us expected anything else from a New Yorker. You're always thinking you are so much better than the rest of us."

All the women look at me and laugh.

With their dirty, makeup smeared faces, the harsh contrasting lights and the strangeness surrounding everything, I feel like I'm in a nightmare or an insane asylum.

I steady myself again by pushing my finger into my palm. It's working, I'm bleeding. I look at these dirty women. I know in my heart, I'm better than them, but I also know that the three of them could take me in a fight, even with Hillbilly chained up. I try to distract myself from causing more trouble and look down at my high-tech alien bracelet. It's black and has some red and green flashing lights, no doubt it's a GPS tracker as much as it's any kind of medical device. Finally, I answer Hillbilly, "I did think it would be enough to let me go. My life matters, I mean look at me and look at all of you. Who's going to miss you from your trashy trailer parks? Your stepfathers or stepbrothers?"

The other three women stop laughing then and look at me with disdain.

I smile back at them. Not a real smile, a bitchy smile. I may be in this terrible situation, but I'm not going to let these women get their laughs at my expense. I watch them out of the corner of my eye to make sure my comments were just enough to shut them up, not attack.

The women are quiet and lost in their own thoughts after merely calling me a 'whore'.

For the next couple of minutes, I wonder if they let my last comment go because my accusations were correct. I can't help but think, *And this is why aliens feel that they can just take us, we don't even take care of each other.*

Countless silent hours pass.

Two green aliens enter the room, it's impossible to tell if these are different from the other ones who have come in before or the same.

They have with them what smells like food, but they have it in one big bowl, not four bowls.

"This is a joke, right?" I can't eat from a bowl with these other women like an animal.

The other women don't answer me, they just move as close as they can to the cage door.

When the bowl is put in, they attack it as if they are ravenous piranha, and I wonder how often we are fed here. I notice that as an afterthought, the other two women give some food to Hillbilly, who's still chained to the wall and they purposely give me a look as to say, and-you-get-none-New-Yorker.

"I don't want any of that. I'm not an animal. It appears you all are right at home here in this cage though," I say while I lean against the cold wall.

The green aliens are watching me. I feel their big black eyes on me. I look at them and one of them gets out his small punishment device.

The same device that had been used to shock me before and probably to levitate me on to the medical bed too. I don't know exactly what the alien's intention is, but I'm pretty sure he wants me to eat from the big communal bowl with the fly-over-states women.

I eye the other women as their feeding has slowed. They feel my eyes on them and look up at me. Without even looking at each other, they move the bowl of food as far away from me as they can.

I slump back against the wall.

The alien with the device shocks me, not as hard as last time, but it isn't pleasant.

I scream a profanity at him and rub my arm.

The alien points to the bowl with his long-gnarled finger.

I look at him and think, *Does he want me to push my way in for food like a savage? Not happening. I'll wait for my own bowl.*

The green alien is annoyed and shocks me again, and this time it hurts more.

It takes me a few seconds to recover from the blow of pain. I'm beginning to see rainbow-colored stars.

The green alien shakes the device at me, never speaking, but it's clear I'm making him annoyed. If he could talk, I'd imagine him saying, 'I've one job, and it's to make sure you all eat. Eat humans.'

I don't want to be shocked again so I move towards the bowl.

The woman from Oklahoma kicks me hard with her dirty bare foot and gives me a nasty look over her shoulder as she continues to shovel in food like a cavewoman, no doubt trying to finish all of it so that there'll be none left for me.

I'm a fighter. My instincts take over. I grab that same foot and bite it as hard as I can. I taste salt, blood and dirt. I'm not squeamish, and I reckon that the blows that'll probably follow from Oklahoma will hurt less than the alien's punishment device. I quickly move up her body, sinking my nails into her cold flesh as I go. I can feel her blood under my nails and hear her grunt with the small pain I'm inflicting.

When I reach her face, I punch her hard like I would any man trying to get too close. I hear her nose crack, followed by a rush of blood. I look at the rest of the women who are looking at me in shock, "Who's from New York now?" I question them.

When they don't answer, I smack the woman from St. Paul across the face, leaving a red handprint and aggressively take the bowl from her. The adrenaline is coursing through my body. I'm ready for anyone to take me on now.

St. Paul smacks me across my face but doesn't try to take the bowl back.

I lean back and kick her as hard as I can in the groin.

She doubles over in pain.

I look in the large bowl, there isn't much food left. It's some kind of cold soya product goop. I eat it with my hands just as the other women had done. I eat it like an animal. I look up at the green alien watching me. He looks the same as he did before, no discernable expression, but I imagine this must be a satisfied look for his species.

After eating, none of us say anything to one another. We try to sleep on and off in the chilly cage. Despite being cold, I refuse to cuddle with any of these women for body heat. I'm not that cold. As far as other amenities go, thankfully, there's a toilet. It's a strange alien toilet that sucks the excrement out rather than waiting for gravity to do its job. It makes a bizarre noise that wakes me every time someone needs to pee, but at least there isn't a bucket in the corner, newspaper on the floor, or anything else primitive. If there had been a bucket for poo and piss, I've no doubt we would have dumped that on one another already with all the fighting going on between us. We are a microcosm of humanity here, but one thing is for sure, I'm fighting to be the alpha.

I'm sure at least a week has passed, maybe more. It's difficult to count the days as every day is the same. We are fed once a day under the watchful eyes of two green aliens, and then we either fight amongst ourselves, or we speculate about our futures. I figure I'll know when a full two weeks have passed as aunt Flo will be paying me a visit, just to make things more fun. That is, only if these green aliens haven't removed my uterus. I've asked the other women about their periods and they haven't gotten them. But we have speculated a number of reasons for us not menstruating besides the aliens having possibly removed our reproductive organs.

"We are definitely not here for medical experiments, or they would have begun those already," I reiterate for the millionth time after a long stretch of silence.

"I might finally begin to agree with you. But it could be the green aliens are only transporting us to the experiment place," Hillbilly scratches her head probably with lice. "And if not, what else could they want with us? They don't have any genitals that I can see. It can't be for sex with them."

"Maybe their nasty bulbous fingers are their sex organs," I suggest and everyone groans. I feel sick now unable to get that image out of my head. I'm relieved when someone changes the subject.

"Maybe we are going to a galactic zoo somewhere?" Oklahoma keeps her eyes on her toes as she talks. She is picking at her overgrown toenails. Her sweet pink toenail polish is almost gone. "I wouldn't mind being well looked after and kept in captivity for curious people to peer in at me from time to time."

St. Paul laughs, "Do you imagine yourself just lounging around getting fat while aliens come to gaze in your cage as a good life?"

Oklahoma frowns, "I could think of a lot worse things that could happen to us right now. So yeah, a nice cage with a constant flow of food sounds good to me."

"Maybe they would even get you a human man for breeding? They'd probably find the most disgusting man you've ever seen. Fat and ugly from captivity. Never having seen a human woman before, he would be let into your cage naked, with his little willy erect and no doubt curved. Then he'd just jump on you like a panting dog, no kissing no caresses just primal, rape, sex while all your zookeepers and curious visitors watched. And it would go on until you conceived. Yes, sounds like a great life," I say sarcastically, thinking about panda bears in captivity. I remember seeing a show about panda bears being shown panda bear porn because the zookeepers wanted the panda bears to get it on and didn't think they knew how to do it.

"It's strange they only took us," Hillbilly says from the corner of the cage. "Do you think they have other prisoners, like children or men in other rooms? Or other animals from Earth?"

"I don't know," I try to remember if I heard any other sounds. "I've not heard anything. Just us the green aliens, clicking, that toilet, us and silence."

Everyone agrees and we drift off into silence again.

The days pass, and the predictable, but uneasy routine continues.

CHAPTER 2

 eb

"You won't be disappointed, Captain Seb. I promise you the best humans. Fresh from Earth. They've passed all of their medical exams and are just waiting to be adopted," the green Dulu peers in too close to his camera on his viewscreen, making me instinctively lean back in my chair.

"Good, I don't like to be disappointed. I've sacrificed half a day to rendezvous with you on the promise that you have a good selection of humans."

"Captain, I promise, you won't be disappointed. I look forward to showing you the women at the meeting point. Mikeal out."

The little green man disappears from my screen, and my first officer sits down across from me, "Dulus are never a hundred percent trustworthy."

"True, but I've wanted a human pet for a while now and I'm not going to wait until we return to the Empire to buy one."

"Of course, you wouldn't be happy with anything less than a human."

"I only want the best," it's prestigious to have a human. They're a fascinating species. Humans are almost genetically the same as Imperial citizens. But, unlike us, humans are barbaric, which makes them a challenge to tame. The real prize in having a trained human is somewhere between having a pet and a conquered loyal companion.

"You're not worried about the rumors that the Imperial Galaxy Court is going to make it illegal to own humans soon?"

"Are you a member of the human rights committee now?" I ask sarcastically.

"Captain, of course, I don't think that humans should have the same rights Imperial citizens or other sentient beings. I only worry about you becoming too attached to your pet and having to give her up if the law is changed. And what about the crew? You know how everyone loves having a human onboard. What would it do to morale if she was taken from us?"

"Stop worrying so much. I don't see that happening. The Empire controls more seats on the IGC than any other species, it's unlikely the law regarding humans will change in our lifetimes. And even if it does, what would we all do with our pets? It's ridiculous. Send them back to Earth? We certainly couldn't send them to our homes in the Empire. No, these thousands of humans lucky enough to leave their backward planet are meant to be pets. They'll live and die onboard our ships, in our quarters. Humans could hardly ask for anything better."

"I guess it's good humans don't live very long, what is it? Sixty years or something?"

"Something like that," I agree casually, but of course, I know for certain how long the average human in captivity lives as I have already spent countless hours researching human pets in preparation for my own.

. . .

TWO HOURS LATER, we board the Dulus' ship. My first officer and doctor accompany me. We are all curious to see these young humans brought directly from Earth. The short green Dulus meet us at the hatch where our two ships are temporarily connected and escort us to their conference room.

The Dulus are weak and slender and had it not been for their superior technology, they would be the lowest slaves in the galaxy. Thankfully, for them, they are more technologically advanced than any other species, and extremely good at business.

"Please, Captain," the Dulu Mikeal says as he ushers us in, "have a seat. I just want to review a few basic guidelines about human pets before we show you and your men our stock. Just to go through the basic process of adopting and the responsibilities of owning a human. I must make sure these humans go to the right kind of owners. It's my reputation as much as it's yours. I don't want to sell a good human to anyone who will mistreat her and then turn around and blame me for bad quality."

"Trust me, I'm the right kind of owner," I'm annoyed that he would even question me, an Imperial captain, but I play along. I want a human pet.

"You may think you are, but you'd be surprised at the returns I get or how often I need to rescue mistreated pets. So, no matter who my clients are, I make sure everyone knows before they buy a human just how much work a human is. It's not like some of the other pets in the galaxy that are easier to tame. But I guarantee you, once you tame your human and form a bond, she'll be more loyal than any other pet in the galaxy," Mikeal says, opening a 3D projection in the middle of the conference room table. He starts showing pictures of various humans, "As you can see, humans come in many different colors and various shapes. But we've found that these are all only cosmetic differences. As for their lifespans, they live only about 60 to 70 Imperial years in captivity; however, human men last only about half of that. The humans I've acquired now are about 20 years old, which means their brains are just now fully developed; however, they are still young enough to be trained and properly tamed. We have found that this is the perfect age to take them, any younger and they are scarred permanently from the trauma of being taken from their homeworld, and any older they are too sad and don't do anything fun. Rest assured, the humans that we trade in are of the best quality and have all been checked for diseases and health. It's up to you whether you want your human to be on birth control or not. As you are from the Empire, I don't really need to tell you about human women's genitals or the birthing process as it's the same for Imperial people. I do, however, need to remind you, though, that no half-breeds are allowed to be sold as pets according to the IGC convention of 4528. If you choose to breed with your pet, you must keep the hybrids at your home and provide for them as you would any Imperial child."

I struggle to keep a smile from my face; his words are so idiotic to my ears, "Yes, I know what to do with the hybrid offspring." The Empire encourages pet offspring. As the Imperial genes are dominant, there is no risk of the human barbarism being passed on and at the same time allows the Empire to keep our gene pool diverse.

"Fine, fine," Mikeal looks around at my men and me. "Any questions for me?"

"I think we are ready to see the humans now," I say, making eye contact with my men. I can see the curiosity in their eyes.

"Let's not waste any more time then," Mikeal rises awkwardly on his thin green legs from his white swivel chair, and his assistants who have been waiting in the hallway meet us and lead us to the cages with the humans for sale.

We pass multiple rooms with other animals from different planets around the galaxy as we make our way down the long hallway. Each room is marked with a different species, and we can see in through one-sided viewers as we pass. As we come upon the humans' room, I give my doctor a grin.

"Here we are," Mikeal says and then opens the door.

When we enter, there are three human women, all physically fighting with one another in their cage at the back of the room. I smile. I didn't expect anything less from the adorable little barbarians.

"Why aren't they in separate cages?" I notice they have bruises and cuts on their different colored bodies.

"Humans like to be together, but they also fight with one another. These humans are fresh and untamed therefore barbarous, but don't worry, those are only superficial wounds. They don't mean to kill each other," Mikeal explains.

We all move closer to the cage. I have only seen a human a few times before and never ones as young and as beautiful as these. Adorably, two humans are pushing another one with the darkest skin to the front of their small cage. She is the strongest of them and has large brown eyes and a swell of hips, the likes of which I have never seen before. Her skin color is comparable to the earth on my home planet, and if I were looking for a human wife, I would choose her. She appears to be the healthiest and I know my doctor will want me to take her, "May I touch them?"

"I wouldn't recommend putting your hand in there now when they are riled up like this," Mikeal says, taking out his circular punishment device. "Let me see if I can get them to settle down. Usually, if I show them this, they obey."

I watch as the human women cower at the sight of the punishment device. I notice that the darker one takes this opportunity to push the yellow-haired one to the front, and now the other two are all pushing her forward. *So much for your taming them*, I think as I watch Mikeal with the humans. At least, I can be sure he hasn't mistreated them, quite the opposite given their reaction.

The yellow-haired human is the smallest of them. I find it charming that she is the one trying to push back now against the other two. I scrutinize her as she pushes with all her might. She has colorful tattoos on her skin, and I wonder if they are permanent. "This one is already marked. Are you sure she's not owned by someone else?"

"No, no. We made sure. Humans like to decorate themselves. Those are flowers from Earth. It's nothing. Are you interested in that one? I can take her out for you if you would like to pet her? She's small but she has spirit and I must admit she is my favorite. Unlike the others she initially tried to reason with us with words. I've never seen that before in a human."

I'm fascinated now, "Yes, take her out."

Mikeal and his assistants use their punishment devices and open the cell.

They half-drag out the yellow-haired human. She is wearing filthy pink and black undergarments to cover her human curves and she is so short, the top of her head only reaches the middle of my chest.

She is defiant in the way she looks up at me.

I pat her messy and dirty hair, intrigued that she has the remnants of a proper braid in it, and it makes me wonder if humans really are on the verge of being somewhat civilized as Imperial people we all braid our long hair. "Come now," I say to her, "Don't look at me like that. Do you want to be my pet? Do you want to go on an Imperial starship?" I can't resist speaking sweetly to her as I find her appearance and face expression curiously charming.

"Can I see all of her, her fur? I thought humans should have more," I ask Mikeal as I step back and look over the little human, holding her arms out by her wrists. She has very little fur under her underarms and I wonder if she is substandard.

Mikeal and his men begin removing the human's undergarments, which she does not like at all. The little yellow-haired human struggles against them, but she's so petite she's no match even for Dulus. In seconds she's naked. She has a magnificent human body with accentuated hips and breasts, but not much fur. The fur she does have is a darker shade of yellow than the hair on her skull, and I find this pleasing. I move closer to stroke what little hair she has covering her sex. It's curled and a bit coarse. I like it. I only wish there was more.

"The fur will grow back in a few weeks," Mikeal speaks authoritatively. "Young women like to trick human men into thinking they are not ready to bear children and remove it. They are all like this when we recruit them. I guarantee you, the fur will grow back. I've been selling humans for over a hundred years now."

I look at the yellow-haired human woman's genitals again. The cutest part about humans is their fur. I'm hesitant as it might not grow back. "And the others' fur? The same?"

Mikeal sighs, "Yes, as I said, they all come this way. It's only to trick human men and it always grows back. You know humanity isn't technologically advanced enough for permanent hair removal. I've never seen it with humans."

I'm silent, considering these three human women. When I imagined my human pet before, I envisioned her having a lot of hair covering her entire vulva, all the way to her anus and under her arms. What I see now is something half human and half Imperial.

"I think you should go for the brownest one. She's the most beautiful and the strongest. The yellow-haired one looks weak," my doctor comments. "Look at the other one's strong body, and she has big breasts and hips. She's the best one here, Captain."

I look over at the third woman, then back at the yellow-haired one standing next to me.

The little one is still looking up at me. I decide her look is insolent and I want to consider one of the others, but I don't want the strongest one. I want a petite human. "Let me see the one with straight black hair."

"She's the most like Imperial people in hair and body shape except her eyes have that adorable almond shape that only some humans have. This kind is incredibly popular with Imperial people. She's, of course, one-hundred percent human, we've done all the tests to prove it and those results will all be transferred with her documents after purchase. I always think these ones support that crazy religious myth you all believe in," Mikeal says as he has his men put the yellow-haired human one back.

I ignore his comment about the religious fundamentalists in the Empire and watch as the straight dark-haired one comes out. She is led in front of me with a punishment device. I pat her head, and then she rewards me by pissing on my leg.

I don't hesitate to slap her down with my hand. "Take her back, she's too much of a savage." I want to change my clothes now that I have human piss on me. "Give me the yellow-haired one," I say reso-lutely. "If she doesn't work out, I'll return her."

"Oh, I'm sure you will get along very well," Mikeal says as he has his associates lead her out of the cage again. They put a blue energy leash around her neck. "She's my favorite. A lot of spirit but quick to learn."

I nod to my doctor, and he begins running his own quick medical check on her. "You don't mind if my doctor checks her to make sure she is healthy, just to be on the safe side. We don't want to buy a sick human or one already carrying a child. And of course, we have our own Imperial protocol."

Mikeal is clearly insulted, "Captain, I assure you I only deal in the highest quality of pets and would never sell you an ill, traumatized, or already pregnant human."

I ignore him. I'm not an idiot. When my doctor nods that the yellow-haired human is in good health, I say to Mikeal, "I believe you now." Then I transfer the UCs with my voice activation code from the UG bank. I make sure to receive a discount due to the piss on my leg. Then I'm given the leash. I look down at the yellow-haired human who is all mine now. "I'm Seb," I point to myself, "Seb." Then I point to her, "Who are you?"

The human looks up at me blankly. I look back at the strong one and wonder if I should switch for that one. I wonder if this one's brain is too small.

"It takes some time," Mikeal explains. "Take her back with you and ask her again after she's had some food." As if reading my mind, he says, "Their brain size has nothing to do with their intelligence, Captain."

We walk back onto my ship. I give the command to separate from the Dulus' ship. I walk through the corridors on my way to my quar-ters and my human pet walks proudly on the leash. Already my concerns about her being overly stupid vanish. Humans are expensive, and it's a status symbol to have one. Everyone we pass stops to admire her. I'm grateful no one mentions her lack of fur. I hope her fur will grow back soon as I don't want to look like I was swindled.

Once we get to my quarters, I take her leash off, "Go over there. That's your place," I say, pointing to a corner with a little bed for a human. I'm disappointed that my human just stands still not doing anything but looking around my quarters. I point again to her place and tell her to go there. She still doesn't understand, so I pick her up gently and put her on her little bed. She seems surprised by my actions. When I set her down, she tries to get up again, but I put my hand on her "Stay."

She tries to get up again, and I put my hand on her again, "Stay." After the fourth time, she understands, and I walk away and watch her out of the corner of my eye.

I open my wardrobe and change my uniform. The material is waterproof so none of the other human's urine touched my skin. I put on fresh trousers, then I take out a human-pet outfit and go back over to my human. Before I dress her, I pick her up and take her into the bathroom.

I voice activate the shower and begin to bathe her.

She screams and tries to run, but I hold her there, getting us both wet while I tell her it's good to get clean. "Hush now, it's good to get you clean. I'm washing all that human dirt from you now. You'll be a spotless Imperial pet now."

I don't think I've ever seen anything as adorable as my human, all wet and covered with soap wearing a frown. All the dirt from her face and body disappear with the water. I can't help but say to her, "Now look how adorable you are now that you're all clean."

I comb her yellow hair while the auto dry does it's work, and then dress her in her new clothes. They are red and consist of a wrap tunic shirt and leggings. She also has little socks and little black boots, all of which I use the universal device to fit her shape. I'm not a shop assistant though so it's not perfect. When she is dressed, I look her over and think she looks adorable. I run my fingers through her yellow hair, I can't help but reiterate, "You are so cute."

She looks up at me then, and I think she might be ready to talk. I'm so excited in anticipation. I try to tell her my name again, "Seb. I'm Seb." Then I point to her, "Who are you? You?"

She just shakes her head at me.

I'm disappointed, but at least she shook her head, that's an improvement. I wonder then if humans shake their head for negation or if that was something she learned from the Dulus. Mikeal said she wasn't stupid, but I have a feeling he'd say anything to make a deal.

Suddenly, I'm called to the bridge, and I look at my little pet, "Go to your place, human."

She just looks at me, bewildered.

I repeat myself three times and point. On the third time, she understands.

I sigh, looking at her in her corner on her little bed, "I'll be back soon. Stay there. Food is coming." Then I reluctantly leave my new pet and at the same time call my squire to join her so that she won't ransack my quarters on her own.

CHAPTER 3

nsley

THE DOOR to our room opens, and for the fourth time new visitors enter. There are only three of us in the cage now. Hillbilly has already been taken. We don't know what for or to where, but one thing is for sure, we are happy we weren't taken by the large, slimy, red octopod looking creatures that took her. After the octopods visited, there were some furry looking aliens, not unlike giant teddy bears but with devilish red eyes. Thankfully, the evil plush toys had no interest in us, no matter how hard the green aliens were trying to sell us to them. Apparently, shaking one's head to mean 'no' is a galactic universal. Next were some seriously freaked-out insectoid type beings. There was no way to tell if they were male or female, but again they wanted nothing to do with us. Which was a big relief, because the large insect beings with all those black eyes and pinchers were possibly the most frightening creatures I'd ever seen in my life.

Now anytime we hear the outer door open and know it's not feeding time, even before we see who is coming into our room, we scurry to the back of the cage and start pushing whoever happens to be slowest to the front, and right now, that is Oklahoma. She's pushing back, but it's two against one. We are all concentrating on pushing as none of us wants to be taken by whatever scary alien thing walks through that door. I'm perfectly happy to stay with the green aliens.

Unluckily, after a few seconds I get caught off guard when one of the green guys brings out his punishment device, and suddenly, I'm the one being pushed up for whatever monster has walked in. My heart is pounding. I'm pushing back as hard as I can to get behind one of the other women and don't even look up at the newcomers even though I can hear their alien language, which sounds vaguely familiar and the green aliens' language too. It was a surprise to all of us the first time we heard the green aliens speak, not only that they could speak but their language sounds like dolphin talk. It became obvious as well they only condescended to talk to their equals, which we clearly were not.

Because I'm right in front now, I'm removed from the cage by two green aliens. I feel like an unlucky goldfish in a tank. I reluctantly allow myself to be walked out and led to whoever is here now. I look up and to my surprise I see a human. He is big and grey, but a human. Relief washes over me.

We make eye contact. He has grey human eyes. I don't speak because the green aliens have made it very clear we are not allowed to speak, or we will be punished. But I'm dying to ask, 'Are you a human in disguise?' He's as tall as a basketball player but is built like a guy on the cover of a hunky romance novel, long black hair and everything. *A grey Fabio*, I think. Quickly I search my heart and decide grey skin isn't a dealbreaker for me consider the other buyers I've seen in here. I turn on my charm. My heart is humming, my eyelashes fluttering, *Pick me! Pick me!* I'm saying with my eyes and body language.

Mr.-Alien-Human-Hottie pets my head as if I'm a puppy.

If I had a tail, I'd wag it. I don't know what Grey Fabio wants me to do. I stand there hoping I'm looking at him with the cutest take-me-home eyes like a puppy in the pound.

He continues to look at me, all the time talking to one of the green aliens like they are making a deal. I like the sound of his voice and his language sounds like it could be German or another European language and again, I wonder, *Is he a part of a secret human rescue group and the grey skin is your camouflage?*

Regardless, my mantra is playing repeatedly in my head, *Please, pick me! Pick me!*

The green aliens take my arms again, and I think they are going to take me away. I struggle, but soon realize they are stripping me. I don't really want to be naked in front of all these people, but then again, what choice do I have? *And does it really matter?* I ask myself. I console myself as I stand there trying to cover my overgrown, itchy bikini line, that at least I'm at least five pounds thinner due to the lack of food.

Mr.-Alien-Human-Hottie runs his fingers through the hair growing back on my vulva and under my arms. I feel embarrassed and he seems displeased. I don't know what to do. *Should I lick him to show him I like him?* I wonder, but before I can even get my tongue out of my mouth, I'm being dragged back to the cage.

When he asks to see St. Paul, I'm disappointed but then ecstatic when she pees all over him like an idiot. He looks angry, and when I'm taken out again I'm thrilled to have an electronic-like leash put on me, I want to say to the two other women, 'See you later bitches,' and 'Have fun with the next octopods who come along,' but I'm wary of the green aliens' punishment devices, so I don't say anything. I just give them a look that means all of that and the middle finger as I'm led out of the room by my handsome grey master.

As I give the human women one last look over my shoulder, they give me the middle finger in return, I stick out my tongue, turn and walk out the door. *So much for the last real humans I might ever see,* I think, and follow my new master off the ship.

As I walk with my new owner, I begin looking these grey men over. They are all dressed alike, all in fitted black uniforms, so I assume they must be a part of a military of some kind. They all have long, I mean, really long black hair in various braids, and they smell like a mixture of leather and woody men's fragrance and freesia women's perfume, like a pleasing, heavy-scented floral soap. I'm relieved to be going with them. *If I'm going to be owned in this galaxy, let my master at least look like me and be clean.*

Once we are on my new master's ship, I notice there are no women, no other aliens and everyone is grey and tall. They all look at me as if I am a cute small doll. *Or puppy*, I remind myself. The ship itself is massive and precisely what I imagine an alien spaceship to look like, kind of dark and with lots of metal and small windows here and there looking out into the vastness of space. I try to stop to look out a window as there weren't any windows that I could see out of on the green aliens' ship, but I'm led away before I can get a good look at open space, which to my surprise actually looks pretty busy.

From the small glimpse I did get, it looks crazy, like an abstract piece of art with lots of colors and clouds on a black backdrop. I want to ask my master if we are somewhere special, but I'm afraid to talk. Part of me is still waiting for him to start speaking English to me and to tell me that they have rescued me. That being grey is only a disguise.

As we continue to walk, I notice the ship is eerily quiet except for shuffle of feet and the low murmur of people talking. I also begin to realize that it is cold. Colder than the green aliens' ship. I hope that my new master is going to give me some clothing. Then I panic and think, *What if I'm meant to be a whore and won't require clothing?* But by the way my master is leading me around his ship, the way his crew caresses the top of my head, and the leash leads me to hope that I am a pet. And I hope fervently that I'm going to be a beloved pet with lots of clothing.

When we reach his quarters, he tries to talk to me in his alien language, but I can't figure any of it out. I'm weary, hungry, and overwhelmed. I just stand there, unsure of what I should do, but still trying to look as cute as I can even though my own appearance must be a fright. The green aliens didn't allow us to bathe so I still had traces of my heavy makeup on my face from weeks ago and my hair is messy and unwashed. I can't even smell myself anymore. Without question, I look and smell like an abandoned puppy that you find in a dirty parking lot.

Suddenly, my master picks me up and sets me down on a small single bed in the corner of his bedroom. The bed is firm. The silky black blankets are both luxurious and soft. It feels great, and even though I'm thrilled at having this little bed to myself, I'm also starving. I need to eat. I assume there must be lots of food available here and probably something better than the cold tofu-like chow the green guys gave us.

My mind starts racing thinking about all the different foodstuffs they probably have on the ship. I get a second burst of energy just thinking about it. Afraid to speak, I try to get up, hoping my master will understand. But he puts his large hand on my shoulder three times to urge me to stay on my bed. When I realize that I'm not going to get any food now, I obediently remain on my bed. I watch him go across the room and grab something then he comes back and picks me up again and takes me to the bathroom. All the time speaking softly to me. It feels strange to be picked up and carried around as it I'm a baby, but I can't deny that I like being held against his strong body and I find comfort in the smell of him and his clean uniform.

We enter a dark yellow stone room. Unexpectedly, water comes from somewhere above me, it's ice cold. I try to bolt, but my master holds me tight. He loosens my braid with one hand, and I try to struggle free of his grip, but it's futile. This big grey man is as strong as if he's made of the same stone in this bathroom. I stop struggling and just begin shivering as an automatic shower robot sprouts from the stone walls and washes me as he continues to hold me in place. I don't break eye contact with my new master throughout my shower. His grey eyes are so human. Once the freezing water stops raining down on me, all I hear is my own teeth chattering in the stone bathroom, but I know my new master has been talking to me in his alien language throughout this ordeal. I'm just too cold to focus.

An automatic body dryer comes on and dries me as my master combs my hair. All I'm hoping for now is some warm clothing, *Please let me be a beloved pet with clothing and not a sex slave for all your crew or random passing aliens.* Throughout my life, I've been lucky. Now I hope that my luck extends to the galaxy as well, *Please let this guy be decent and not an alien sadist.*

My master sets me in the middle of the room and goes to his wardrobe. I can't see into the wardrobe from where I am standing, but I'm relieved when he returns with clothes and shoes for me. They are both warm and comfortable. And most importantly, they cover everything that would usually be covered. Of course, I would've loved a bra and underwear, but you can't have everything.

I remind myself that at least I'm not with some evil red-eyed teddy bears or slimy octopods. I doubt that Hillbilly got any clothing. I hope for her sake she didn't live long. I sigh, pitying her, thinking her whole life must have been so tragic. I hope that she did a lot of meth in her short life to escape it all. Then I suppress a shudder thinking about all those gooey tentacles going places I'd never want tentacles to go and hope again she met a quick end.

Once I'm dressed, my master begins talking to someone in his alien language, but I don't see or hear anyone replying. Nor do I see him get out a phone or anything. *I hope he isn't insane*, the thought crosses my mind as I watch him. After he finishes talking, he looks at me, and then my new master tries to tell me something again.

I'm trying to listen to his words and understand, but I can't make heads or tails of it.

Then, without warning, he picks me up again and puts me on my little bed gently.

I try to get up again. I want food. *Why can't he see that I'm hungry?* I wonder.

He puts his steady hand on my shoulder, making it clear I should stay.

I put my hand on my stomach and then look up at him with the biggest hungriest eyes I can manage, but he just pats my head.

I watch him leave the room. I decide that when I think he's been gone long enough, I'm going to rummage through his quarters and see if I can find any food. After the food, I'll look for anything to get me home or at least find out where I am and with whom.

Just as I think it might be safe to begin snooping around, exhaustion takes over and I fall into a deep sleep on the soft and silky bed surrounded by my own wonderfully alien perfumed body and hair.

I wake up to my master, gently petting my hair and talking to me softly.

I open my eyes and look directly into his grey ones. I can't help but think again, *Are you human?* I try to listen to his words as I'm more alert now than I have been in weeks, but I still have no idea what he is saying.

I slowly sit up and survey the room, then look back at him. I think he must realize that I don't understand because he picks me up and sets me down in a chair at a white table in front of a dish of warm food. I look up at him, not knowing if he wants me to eat this with my hands like the green aliens or what.

He's looking at me all mystified.

I decide since he hasn't left the bowl on the floor that he wants me to eat like a civilized being. I curiously investigate the strange cutlery he has now pointed out to me on the side of the black ceramic dish, and I smell the food that looks like something between rice and porridge, it doesn't have a particular smell other than carbs with a capital 'C'. I pick up what I would call a large and very thin metal spork and begin eating the food. The food is bland but not disgusting. I eat everything. Then I look at my new master for more food. I even hold up my dish like Oliver Twist, but he replies with such a distinct tone, I know there'll be no more food right now. I frown hoping he hasn't got me on a diet. I'm not the kind of girl who likes to be hungry.

I want to get up from the table, but my master is sitting across from me staring. I don't move. I don't know what he wants, but I want to please him just in case all of this is a façade and he really is a torturer and killer of humans if he is angered. I return his gaze the entire time, wondering what he has planned for me. I've never had anyone look at me the way he is now. It's something between adoration and curiosity. I don't want to disappoint him, so I simply sit. The longer we sit in silence staring at each other, the more crazy ideas begin to trickle into my mind, like maybe he has only been pretending to be kind, and now that he has fed me, it's all going to turn really terrible. I wonder if I'm going to be put in some gladiatorial ring and have to fight other aliens to the death. I try to stop my mind from running with all of these hypothetical situations because I'm scaring myself, but I can't seem to stop this river of horrendous scenarios running through my mind. After a while, I gather my courage to stand. I slowly stand up from the table, never breaking eye contact with him.

My master stands with me, leaves the table, and returns with my leash.

I watch him while he attaches it around my neck. As I look at him, I ponder what he would look like if he had human skin. I look at his facial features, but none of them reveal any generalizations of any human ethnicities. He simply looks human. His grey eyes meet mine, and then he pats me on the head and leads me out of his quarters on a walk around the dark ship.

This time he allows me to stop and look out the large passing windows when I want to. I'm curious. I want to ask him where we are and why there are so many colors in space, but obviously, I don't have the words that he would understand. As I look out at a mass of colors in space, I wish I'd studied more astronomy in school, unfortunately I'd been more interested in astrology than astronomy.

It occurs to me that I don't even know if I'm still in the Milky Way. For some reason, this makes me dizzy and my palms go clammy because this is another reminder of my helpless state. That I'm the equivalent to a baby left out in a busy city with no way to walk, talk, read or get myself home. I turn and look at my master again; he's just watching me strangely, and for the first time, I wonder, *Is this a parallel universe where humans are big and grey? And that this is the Milky Way, but it's backwards?* I'm no scientist, but I find it unlikely that there would be two species that are almost exactly the same in one galaxy. I start breathing faster and I put my hand on my chest to try and physically make myself stop. I hate it when my mind takes off down ridiculous tangents just to scare me.

I close my eyes, trying not to become overwhelmed with such a crazy thought of being stuck on the other side of a parallel universe. I can deal with alien abductions, those seem plausible, but a parallel universe makes me want to vomit because I can, theoretically, find a spaceship home, but I can't even conceive how I would get back from a parallel universe.

I feel my master's cold hand on my naked arm.

I open my eyes and try to calm myself.

My master pets me and says some alien words to me, pointing out into space.

I don't know what he's saying, but it sounds reassuring, and I force myself to think, *This is an alien abduction nothing more.* The thought of a parallel universe alarms me, not just because I wouldn't know how to return to Earth, but because its very existence would mean that I don't really matter and that none of this, what I think is reality, matters. That maybe we really are just different computer programs being run for the amusement of higher beings. Just different lab rats or entertainment compartments for god-like creatures we can't see.

As I like to do with other unpleasant ideas, I push it to the back of my mind and imagine boxing it up, just like the Ark of the Covenant and pressing this thought down in my mind with a big sign that reads, 'Ensley's-anxious-thoughts-classified'.

I take a deep breath.

My master pulls on my leash as he begins walking again and I follow.

After walking for a few minutes, we enter a room, not unlike a large private dining room.

There are five other large grey alien men there. My master sits down in a chair, and he indicates that I should sit at his feet. I do, and it's not long before I'm lulled to sleep by their strange alien conversation, my head pressed against the soft black uniform covering my master's ridiculously strong calf. His large hand petting my head, making me feel safe.

As I lose consciousness, I think about the alien language I'm hearing all around me and realize that it has all the sounds of English, but there are no similar words, only sounds that sometimes sound like they might be a word I recognize, but then it's not. The rhythm is so strange, but not unpleasant. I hear one word again and again, and I think *This word must be 'yes' or some kind of agreement*. And that's the last thought I have as I drift off to sleep.

When my master and his friends are finished eating, my master wakes me, bids me to stand up and walk around the room. His friends also stand, and they all watch me, circling me. They are so big and I'm so small. I feel scared. They begin to pet me. At first, it's just on my head and back, but then they begin to touch other parts of my body. I don't like this, I'm worried that they might gang rape me. I back away and instinctually say as confidently and as loudly as I can, "Don't touch me."

All the men, including my master, are stunned by my verbal outburst, but after a second of surprised silence, they smile at me and begin happily talking around me.

I'm relieved that they didn't beat me down for speaking or worse, start raping me. It occurs to me that they are charmed by my talking. I can't help but think, *Oh my God, I'm a talking pet*.

Two of the younger men obviously wanted to try their luck again, and one of them grabs my crotch, "Stop touching me!"

I try to go into the fetal position on the floor so they will leave me alone.

But just as they begin to pick me up, I hear my master scolding them. He comes and picks me up gently. He smells so lovely, and I feel safe with him now, my body pressed against his chest. He says something softly to me, resumes sitting in his chair, still holding me, and the men continue talking and drinking what I assume must be something like wine.

I eye the wine in front of me on the table. There's nothing I want more than to have some. I look up at my master, but he isn't paying attention to me. I reach one of my hands out for his large black cup. As soon as my hand is on it, all the conversation stops, and everyone at the table is looking at me.

My master puts one of his large cool grey hands over mine. I can feel his cold silver rings on the back of my hand and he silently pries my fingers off the cup.

I look up at him pleadingly, "Master, I'd like some wine."

Of course, he has no idea what I've said and doesn't reply. He takes both my hands in one of his large ones and holds them in my lap. With his free hand, he drinks his wine, not looking back at me.

I console myself that it could be worse, and I close my eyes in defeat. While I lay cradled in my master's lap, I resign myself to my new life as his sober human pet. I smile, wondering if I will get the alien equivalent of a pet name too, like 'Princess', 'Bella' or 'Bam-Bam.' If I could chose, I think 'Bam-Bam' would be the best pet name for me. I think about this and other non-important things while the men talk and I'm cuddled in my master's lap.

I barely wake later as my master puts me into my bed in his quarters. He takes off all my clothing. I tense worrying he's going to rape me, but he does nothing of the sort, he simply tucks me into my luxurious bed and leaves me. I hear him strip off his own clothing in the dark and get into his large bed not far from mine. That's it. He doesn't even snore.

I lie awake in the silent darkness, wondering what my future will be and how long my life will be like this. I hope that I've won the alien pet lottery and that I'll stay with this master forever. I imagine my days will be like this, that he bathes me, feeds me and pets me. I assume all I need to do is be loyal then I correct myself, *I hope all I need to do is be loyal like a puppy.* I fall asleep thinking, *I can be loyal.*

The next morning, I awake to find another grey person, a young man, gently tapping my nose.

He speaks to me, although I don't understand his words, it's clear that he wants me to get up.

I follow him to the bathroom.

As we enter he uses words to activate the toilet out of nowhere in the stone wall and then, without my being ready for it, he picks me up and puts me on it as if I wouldn't know what a toilet was or how to use it.

Even though I know it's ridiculous to speak to the young man because he can't understand me, I can't resist and say haughtily, "Master told me how to use the toilet yesterday." This is a lie, of course, but I assume he's also a servant of some kind and I don't want him to think he's better than me.

The young man jumps at the sound of my voice and that makes me smile. Then he gives me a look that I interpret as, I-don't-want-to-take-any-chances.

I give the young man a look of disdain in reply, but he merely shrugs while he watches me pee.

It's strange, I reflect. *I'm beyond caring about being naked and an alien young man watching me pee.* I'm sure he would have wiped me too if the toilet hadn't done that for him and what's worse is that I probably would have let him because I do like to be pampered.

Next, the young man lifts me up in front of the bathroom mirror he has activated and takes out a green laser.

I'm so frightened by the laser, I try to run away, but he grabs me forcefully and holds open my mouth as he brushes my teeth. The laser feels warm and tingly, with the taste of black licorice. I don't like the taste of black licorice, but there's no way I can get out of his grip. All I can hope is that the taste like toothpaste will fade with the day.

The young man then ushers me out of the bathroom and leaves me standing in the middle of my master's quarters naked while he goes to get clothes for me. I assume I'll wear the same outfit as yesterday, but apparently, my master is a shopper, as I notice from this vantage point, he has a lot of clothes for me in his closet next to his uniforms. I wonder then if he has owned a human pet before me, and then I panic wondering what happened to her and if he might have killed her or thrown her out an airlock, which happens a lot in space movies. I'm dying to ask the young man, but there's no way for me to ask without words in his language. I promise myself when I get a chance, I'll snoop through the room for any evidence of a pet or pets before me. I want to survive this.

The young man returns to where I'm standing and dresses me in navy blue trousers, with matching boots and a black long-sleeved shirt that again crosses in the front. Next, I'm guided to the table and he bids me sit.

I do. Then I wait. It isn't long before food on a black plate is set in front of me. It's similar to what I had yesterday, and I eat it with the strange spork cutlery. I'm only given water to drink.

The young man sits across from me, watching me just as my master had done.

I finish all my food and ask for more by lifting up my empty plate.

To my delight the young man nods and gives me more.

I smile at the young man and think, *You and I will be good friends.* When I finish my third helping and feel full for the first time since I left Earth. All I want to do is go back to my little bed and sleep a fat lazy sleep. I stand and gingerly walk towards my bed.

But the young man has different plans. He takes my wrist, puts my leash around my neck, and leads me out of my master's quarters without a word.

When we have walked around the ship at least three times, I realize he's seriously walking me, as you would walk a dog. I would rather be sleeping but at least the young man lets me walk slowly and stops often to let members of the crew pet my hair and speak to me as if I'm an adorable pet. Even though, I've no idea what they are saying, their tone is warm and friendly.

Don't get me wrong, all of this is humiliating, but I remind myself over and over again how much worse it could have been. I constantly tell myself, *I could have been taken like Hillbilly.* And my mind wanders to the other women too, I wonder if they are as lucky as I am or if they are with even worse aliens than the few I saw.

After four times around the ship, I'm taken to my master, who isn't in his quarters but in a room I've not been into before. As we enter and I look around, I summarize this is a large conference room complete with 3D computer projections. My eyes scan the readouts, but I can't even identify any numbers, let alone words. I'm happy to suppose then, *In a parallel universe they'd probably use Arabic numerals.* I don't know why I assume this, but it makes me feel secure in my belief that I'm merely a victim of an alien abduction.

As I tear my eyes away from the alien projections hovering above the table and look around the room, I realize that my master must be important because he is sitting at the end of the table. The rest of the men are around the table, intently listening to whatever he's saying.

When my master finishes talking, his face expression changes from serious to jovial when his eyes meet mine.

I could slap myself as his expression makes me happy too, and I smile. I wonder if pets have unconditional love for their masters simply because being in a home is so much better than being in the puppy pound.

My master comes over and takes my leash from the young man. This also makes me ridiculously happy, and I swear it's the strangest thing in the world, I'm pleased to be following him around the room while he continues to speak his alien language while the other aliens watch us both circle the large table. My master is important, and it makes me feel important.

After he finishes speaking, some of his men get up and come over to pet me. They all have cool hands, and I conclude that these grey men must have lower body temperatures than humans, which is why the food is only lukewarm, the shower is cold, and the ship is cold because all of this is only cold for me.

After the grey alien meet and greet, my master gives my leash back to the young man, and then he takes me back to my master's quarters. Once there, he takes off my leash and all my clothing and says something and points to my bed. *Okay,* I think, *I guess it's finally nap time.* I don't mind as I want a chance to look around my master's quarters. I get into the soft bed and pretend to go to sleep. I'm hoping the young man will leave, but every time I open one of my eyes, he's still there in the chair watching me. After a while, I realize that he isn't going anywhere, so I close my eyes and try to sleep in earnest.

My master wakes me up when he comes in. I assume he's off-duty now. I don't know what he says, but at the sound of his voice, I open my eyes.

I sit up, and then I swear he calls to me in his alien language, and I know it and go to him, naked. All the while thinking *This is ridiculous.* But he's pleased, pats my head and looks at me so adoringly.

After petting me, he just looks at me for a few seconds, then he points to himself and says something and then points to me.

I finally figure out he is telling me his name or how to say 'master' or something.

I say the word "Seb."

He's genuinely thrilled with me now and he keeps pointing to me.

As I'm his pet, I assume he would give me a name, but it seems like he actually wants my real name, so I point to myself, "Ensley."

He repeats my name, making sure.

He has an accent when he says my name because he's putting the stress on the wrong syllable. But I find the way he says my name charming. A thought then occurs to me, *Maybe I'm meant to be a pet and it's my true destiny.* But I shoo that thought away, *No, I'm a feminist. I'm just making do the best I can in this alien abduction situation.*

I point to myself again, "Ensley". And then point to him and say, "Seb."

My master, Seb, seems elated by this little linguistic exchange and begins merrily talking in a wild burst of alien language that I don't comprehend, but he uses my name a few times and looks delighted. So I smile back.

Seb quickly dresses me in the clothing I had been wearing before and then puts my leash on and begins leading me out. I wonder where we are going. But soon enough, we are in what I supposed is the ship's sickbay. There are what looks like doctors, injured grey aliens, and medical things. I definitely don't want to go in. I don't even like doctors on Earth. I'm absolutely not going into an alien medical center willingly. I stand my ground at the entrance and pull back on my leash.

Seb is having none of this. He simply says something in his alien language, picks me up and carries me in.

I try to crawl on down his back, but he holds on to me tightly so I can't get away. I feel the vibration of him speaking to someone, and then he lays me down on a medical bed and holds me there.

Another alien is looking over me. He's speaking in the alien language, but surprisingly he uses my name too. Then he begins running a machine over me with a light.

I'm scared.

I look up at Seb and say his name and nothing more. I don't want any alien jelly put in my mouth like last time.

Seb pats my head and makes a sharp 'Zzz' sound, which I assume must just be the reassuring sound in his language. Then he and the doctor speak to each other over me.

I try to get up and get away, I don't like being in the medical center, but Seb takes me and holds me to him again. This makes me feel somewhat safe. He isn't going to let the doctor do any crazy medical experiments on me. Soon we are walking out, and when we get a reasonable distance from the medical center, Seb puts me down and leads me by my leash again.

As we walk, I hope we are going back to his quarters, but soon I realize that we aren't. We are walking towards a door I recognize. It's a door that takes us off the ship. Again, I don't want to go, and I begin verbally saying, "No," and shaking my head, which I know he understands. I don't want to be traded to someone else. I want to stay with him. I know he doesn't understand my words, but I keep trying to tell him, "No, I want to stay here with you. Seb, please. Don't sell me."

* * *

Seb

I'm THRILLED my little human has finally said my name and now I know hers as well. It's the first step of her learning the Imperial language which is important for basic communication.

I took her to the doctor to see if I could get her a translation chip. I read in 'Pets in the Galaxy' that some humans have them and have not become psychotic from the implant. However, my doctor doesn't think it's a good idea. He says that humans are too emotional to be able to benefit from so much logical technology and that it's better if my pet learns our language the natural way. Of course, I'm disappointed as this will take a very long time, but today we passed the first step, she understands my name and I hers.

I like her name, 'Ensley,' it's so cute and human. It suits her very well. I could have given her a typical human pet name like 'Bola' or 'Terai,' but I'm glad to call her by her real name, it's part of the charm of having a human pet.

Now we are docked at Fuloir Station. It's a huge trading port. There is a shop here that specializes in human-pet clothing and another shop with human pet food. I want to take Ensley to buy her more clothing for after her settling-in stage, and human foodstuffs that she might like as a treat. I've been warned though that humans are so barbaric that they can overindulge themselves in everything, not just sex, which is the most commonly known excess in humans. But Ensley didn't fight me when I refused her more food, so I believe she doesn't want to overeat, and therefore, I feel confident there is no risk in her becoming fat.

However, at the moment, we are caught at the exit to the ship. She's speaking human and it's clear she's scared to leave. It's frustrating that she can't communicate and doesn't trust me. Still, I can't be too upset with her as she has only been with me for a few days, and I don't know how she was really treated by Mikeal and his crew or how terrible her life was on the human planet humans stupidly call, 'Earth.' I know that humans are barbarians, so I'm patient with her, and I know it's wrong to cuddle her so much, but I can't help myself when I see her frightened expression. I have to pick her up to comfort her soft and petite frame.

And now that she is clean, she smells divine. I like holding her, and I'm pleased that despite her fear, she doesn't cry or whine or make too much noise. I've seen other humans that cry, and I think I might find that annoying.

Now, as usual, with all the new places I have taken my pet to, I've had to pick her up and carry her, and walking into the station has been no different. I wonder if she is timid by nature or if this is normal human behavior. None of the research I have done about human pets mentioned this. However, I'm confident that when we get to the human shop, and she realizes where we are, she'll be happy. If she's lucky, there might even be some other humans for her to play with for a little while. I know that it's important that humans socialize with each other frequently.

As I walk through the busy station carrying Ensley, I look down and notice her big eyes.

She's not trembling, but she is frightened. I decide at that moment that I'll just carry her all the way to the shop. It's no good if she gets too scared now and pees all over herself and then can't enjoy the store.

As we enter the human shop, I put Ensley down and tell her to look around. I motion with my hand that she can touch things. She does, but it doesn't seem like she knows what she is looking at, and after a second, she just stands there confused. But then I see her eyes lock with another human's, and she starts pulling her leash towards the other pet. I allow this because I want her to feel comfortable. I only hope that the other pet can talk to her and has a good owner.

I've heard that humans all still have different languages, so they can't all talk to one another. I have also heard that some people treat their pets terribly. The last thing I would want to happen now is for Ensley to fear me, but I figure, as we are in the human-pet store, I'm probably not going to meet anyone who mistreats their pet here.

As we get closer to the other human pet, I see the pet's owner is an Imperial admiral. I bow to him, and we begin talking about our humans.

"I just acquired her a few days ago. She is still settling in. And yours?" I ask curiously, eyeing his older human who I suspect might have an eating problem.

"This is Maria. She's been with me for a long time now, twenty years, that's forty years to them, you know?"

I smile, "And any offspring?"

"A few, they are traders and quite content with their lives. They completely pass for Imperial, though, and I would have just claimed them as my own if my wife would have let me. What does your wife think about your human?"

"My wife had an accident and is with the goddess now."

"Peace to those in death," the Admiral says, and I bow acknowledgment.

"It's probably better that you'll be looking for a new wife after you already have your pet, then she will know beforehand."

"Yes," I say, but to be honest, I still miss my wife and feel the heaviness of the tragedy. I don't know if I can ever marry again, but this isn't something I can speak about openly to anyone. It's everyone's duty to the Empire to marry and have children. "How about this shop?" I ask, wanting to change the subject. "Does your pet like it? Have you been here before?"

"This shop is fine, but there is an even better one on Koipo Station with a large human play area. I reward Maria by taking her there sometimes. She loves it."

I look down at Ensley and tell her, "You can talk to her." Then I look back up at the Admiral, "I think she's a little shy."

The Admiral looks at his pet, "Maria, speak to this pet."

To my surprise, Maria answers in almost perfect Imperial, "I already said 'hello' to her. She doesn't speak my human language, and I don't speak hers."

The Admiral looks at me with sympathy, "Oh that's too bad. There's a small play area in the back, maybe you should take her there, and she can find someone who speaks her language." Then he asks Maria, "Is her language rare?"

"No, it's common, just not mine. Your pet only has a few words in mine, and they are of no use in this situation."

I wonder what those words might be if they aren't useful in this situation and in what situation those few words would be helpful in. I can't help but think dark thoughts for my Ensley then, but before I can question the other pet more, they say their goodbyes. I look down at Ensley and say unnecessarily, "Let's go to the play area."

I lead her to the back of the shop where there is a small enclosed well-guarded area where you can let your pet interact with other humans. I look in and am surprised to see a human male there among the women and I'm suddenly unsure about letting my Ensley go free in the pet play area. I don't want her to be raped by the male.

The shop assistant whose responsibility it is to oversee the play area assures me that the male is well-behaved and doesn't pounce on any of the females.

I nod and I take off Ensley's leash and let her go into the enclosure. I don't leave though. I stand outside like an overprotective owner because I don't want anything bad to happen to her. I'm worried about her. Only moments before she was so scared in my arms walking through the station and what if these other pets attack her? But then I remember her and the other women fighting in Mikeal's cage, and I'm curious to see how she will react to these other pets now that she has been given a good home. I'm confused about her nature, is she so different with me than she is to other humans.

Ensley stands at the entrance to the play area, unsure of what to do. She looks at me. I assure her with some hand gestures that I'll be here and to go and have fun.

In the play area a handful of humans are talking, playing with balls, swinging on swings, or playing in a small pool of water. I watch Ensley tentatively walk up to a small group of human women, but unfortunately for her, they don't want to talk to her and make her go away by shaking their heads at her. I feel pity for my pet and I imme-diately want to pull her out as obviously she's distressed that those pets don't want to play with her. Then she tries again with another group, and they also turn her away.

I'm just about ready to call her back to me when I see the male come up to her. I don't want him talking to her, but she doesn't seem scared, so I tensely watch. Ready to leap in and save her if he tries anything. The human male seems only to be talking to her and keeping his distance, and Ensley looks pleased with this. I watch her and the male talk for some time, and then they play with a ball, kicking it back and forth, and I'm glad she gets some playtime with another pet and someone who obviously speaks her language.

More than ever, I realize she must learn Imperial not just to communicate with me but with other pets. She can't live a full life if she can't socialize with her own kind.

When I'm confident that Ensley won't be harmed in the play area, I look around the shop for some clothes for her. I have some already, but they are not explicitly suited to her as I didn't know what kind of human I'd buy. Now that I know, I want to buy clothing specifically for Ensley. I walk around the shop and choose lots of things I hope she will like, and when I retrieve her from the play area, I'll have her put them on and allow the shop assistant to adjust them to her small size.

After I finish with my clothing selections, I return to the play area and call for Ensley at the door. She reluctantly comes to me, and I put her leash back on her. I lead her to the fitting rooms where I help her with a shop assistant to try on the new clothing. I'm naively surprised that when we enter the fitting rooms, there is another human pet with the shop assistant, and she's conveniently there to talk to the other pets. I think to myself, *We should have come here first.*

When the other pet approaches Ensley, it's clear that again they can't speak to one another, and I'm disappointed. The shop assistant's pet tells me, "She doesn't speak my language, and I only speak a little of hers, but I'll do the best I can."

I'm a little excited at the idea that this pet can communicate with my Ensley at all as I'm curious to know her thoughts.

We are ushered into a dressing room and I begin removing Ensley's clothing. Again, I notice that she is shy and doesn't want to take off her clothing in front of so many people, I try to reassure her that it is all okay both by speaking to her calmly and patting her head. I'm surprised when the other human pet, I assume translates my words, because then Ensley looks up and speaks back to me in her own language. I don't know what she says, but she looks so sweet and earnest I can't help but be charmed.

The shop assistant's pet says, "She doesn't like to show her body to strangers."

I pet her head again, "Tell her it's okay. I'm here and I won't let anything bad happen to her." All I can think is that my poor Ensley must have had a terrible life on Earth and that barbarian men have tried or succeeded in raping her, and that is why she is so afraid to show her sex to anyone. I've read that animalistic instincts still guide most of human culture and that humans are incapable of controlling their desires for anything pleasurable.

I remove Ensley's clothing and begin to put the new clothing on her. We are all quiet except for the sporadic talk between the shop assistant and myself discussing sizes and fit of pet clothing. I can't help but notice that Ensley stares at herself in the mirror with the new clothing and I wonder what she is thinking about. She looks neither happy nor sad.

When Ensley is dressed in one of her new outfits, I think she looks stunning, and as the shop assistant begins to fit the clothing, I ask her about the human fur, "Will the fur between her legs grow back?" I'm already so fond of Ensley, I wouldn't get rid of her even if she never has anymore fur between her legs or under her arms.

The shop assistant's pet asks Ensley, she replies and translates, "Yes. However, she says she doesn't want to wear this. I tell her she must, but I don't have the words to explain it to her adequately."

I look at Ensley, our eyes meeting in the reflection of the mirror. I caress her vulva, "Good human." Hoping that this will make some sense to her.

The shop assistant translates my words.

Ensley gives me a confused look and puts her hands over her exposed vulva.

I move her hands away and say, "No."

The shop assistant's pet translates and then Ensley puts her head down.

I wonder if she is going to cry, but when she raises her head again, she looks at me with anger. I smack her vulva, not too hard, but enough for her to know my displeasure, "Bad human."

The shop assistant's pet translates my words and then Ensley looks up and smiles at me.

I don't know what to do now. *Is she mad?* "Why is she smiling?" I ask the shop assistant's pet.

"I don't know. I can't speak her language well enough. Maybe I've translated something wrong."

I can see the shop assistant's pet smirk and I wonder what kind of human pet nonsense is transpiring. However, her smirk disappears so I decide she must have translated something wrong and is embarrassed by her own mistake. I'm confident that Ensley will learn how to be a good pet. This is the first time she has acted outwardly disobediently. I make Ensley try the rest of the clothes which are much more attractive and suited to her human figure.

After an hour and lots of UCs spent, I lead Ensley out of the pet clothing store and to the human food store. As we enter and I see many other human pets out with their owners. Ensley makes no movements to talk to any of the pets. I pat her yellow hair, "Ensley, you can speak to some of the other pets. You won't see another human for a long time, we are going way out into no man's land into the galaxy." I also use a hand gesture to show her she can go lead me to other pets she might want to talk to. I feel sorry for Ensley because I know she doesn't understand what I'm saying to her and by the time she does understand it will have been months since she will have seen another human.

Ensley just looks up at me in bewilderment.

I pat her head again, letting her know that it's okay and ask her, "What kind of food do you prefer?" I point to some things that I hope she recognizes. The store, of course, only has examples on the shelves to save space, but Ensley doesn't seem to recognize anything. I walk to the front of the shop in search of some help.

I'm pleased to see there is another little play area for humans near the collection point.

I look at Ensley and she looks up at me, "Ensley, do you want to go play?" I point to the area with a few human females there.

Ensley looked up at me with her big green eyes, "Seb."

That's all she says, and I assume that means she wanted to stay with me. I stroke her hair, "You don't have to."

Soon a shop assistant comes over and I explain my situation, "I just acquired this human and she doesn't speak Imperial yet. I don't know what she prefers to eat. Do you have a pet to speak to her or is there something all humans like that I could purchase?"

The shop assistant calls to her pet and a bounding human with long red hair comes over.

She's big, older, jovial, and speaks perfect Imperial, "How can I help?"

I'm astounded that she would speak to me so directly without her owner's permission first, but I'm new to the human-pet world, so I let this breach of formality go, "Please ask my pet what she likes to eat."

The shop assistant's pet looks at Ensley and speaks to her in a human language. Suddenly I see my Ensley come to life as I have never witnessed before.

The two human women are chatting for a good few minutes before the shop assistant's pet informs me, "She doesn't understand why she needs food from here."

"Tell her we are going far away, and there will only be Imperial food for a very long time."

The shop assistant nods and translates this to Ensley, and they continued to talk for another few minutes. I'm happy for Ensley that she has finally found someone who speaks her language on the station, but I'm also frustrated not being able to understand what she wants myself. I interrupt the humans, "What is she saying?"

The shop assistant's pet looks up at me, "She doesn't know what food to buy. A lot of this food is from an area of Earth she is unfamiliar with. Most human pets come from the southern hemisphere and she is from the northern hemisphere."

I sense the shop assistant's pet is probably lying to me as I cannot imagine Earth being so complicated in their cuisine, but there isn't any way for me to know. Earth and the Solar System, as they ignorantly call their galactic neighborhood, is off-limits and because of that our official Imperial translators don't translate any of their human languages. "Tell her if she doesn't want any human food from here, we will go."

The shop assistant's pet translates this quickly and replies to me formally, "Please Captain, your pet really wants human food, she thanks you for your patience and kindness and wants me to explain things to her. I know that she will recognize things when I explain our products to her and tell her how this food was acquired. It's confusing for a lot of pets, you know. We don't know about the rest of the galaxy until we are here."

I nod, and I let the pets lead and I follow with the shop assistant. Ensley is still on her leash, although I notice that none of the shop assistants' pets are on leashes, and I wonder if I will ever train Ensley so well to allow her such freedom. At the moment, I can't ever imagine it, not because of loyalty issues, but because she seems so little and shy. I only want to keep her close to me and protect her. Even next to the other human with red hair, she seems small and vulnerable.

The shop assistants' pet has a little tablet out and I'm shocked, "Your pet can read Imperial?"

Instead of the shop assistant replying, the red-haired pet does, which is again odd, but I'm intrigued, "Yes, my master taught me so that I can help out more in the store. I love being able to help."

After she answered my question the shop assistant gave her a small brown morsel of food and the red-haired woman beamed. "What was that you gave her?"

"It's called chocolate. Humans love it. You should buy a lot; it helps with the training."

I want to ask if she's worried about her human pet getting fat, but I realize she probably doesn't care because her human pet is already overweight. I want to find out if it's the chocolate that makes them fat, but I also want to be diplomatic, "Does your pet like to eat a lot, or just chocolate?"

I'm relieved when the shop assistant smiles at me. "Oh Captain, I can see this is your first pet. Don't worry, just like us, they only become fat if you overindulge them, and I must admit, Hannah is such a good pet I can't deny her. Chocolate treats won't make your pet fat as long as you only reward her in moderation. But it's just so difficult, humans love these treats so much and they are so cute."

"I see," I reply. "Please ask my pet if she likes chocolate, if she even knows what it is." I watch the red-haired pet ask Ensley and see her face light up. I'm happy about this and decide I will buy a lot of chocolate for her but unlike this sales assistant I will not allow my pet to overindulge.

We continue to walk through the shop as the pets continually chat in their human language. I assume they are only talking about food as the red-haired shop assistant is doing most of the talking. There is so much I want to know about Ensley, but I can't ask the shop assistant's pet to translate. I don't want anyone knowing anything personal about my pet. She is mine.

When we reach the collection point, and a robot has been sent to retrieve the goods we want to buy, the red-haired human asks me, "Your pet wants to know how long until she can come here again?"

I look at Ensley, "About a year, two Earth years."

The shop assistant's pet tells Ensley.

"She wants to know if we can triple this order?"

I nod.

"She wants to know if she can have wine."

I look at Ensley, "No, alcohol is poison and is not for pets." I speak to her gently. I wonder again about what kind of horrible life she must have endured on Earth.

The red-haired pet translates what I have said to Ensley and I can see she is disappointed. I pat her head.

As we are waiting, the red-haired pet asks me, "She wants to know why you want her to wear the crotchless clothing."

"Because I want her to look as best as she can. Not only is she my pet, but she is morale for the crew."

The shop assistant's pet translates this and there's a lot of shaking heads between the two humans.

"Ensley wants to know if it will be painful," the shop assistant's pet asks.

"Not unless she is naughty," I reply seriously looking down at Ensley. I can't read her face expression and I wonder then how 'morale' was translated.

The shop assistant translates my last words.

Then, Ensley gives me a look of disbelief as if I have said something cruel.

"Tell her I don't expect her to be naughty."

The shop assistant's pet tells Ensley, and they discuss this for a few minutes.

Then, out-of-the-blue, the shop assistant's pet teaches Ensley how to say 'yes' in Imperial.

Ensley looks up at me and says, "Yes, Seb," and this makes me ecstatic. So happy, in fact, by the time it comes to pay, I buy Ensley everything she wants, and have it sent ahead to the ship.

As we walk out of the human food shop, I want to make one final stop at the jewelry store. I know it isn't usual to buy human pets jewelry, but I want something for my Ensley.

She looks so plain without anything.

I lead her into one of the many jewelry shops on the station that advertise they carry everything. I assume that means some pet jewelry too.

Two shop assistants come out to greet me, "How may we help you today, Captain? Something for your wife?" I'm not known to these assistants, but they give me the respect my uniform dictates, and it makes me feel comfortable. It was a little unnerving to have so many human pets speaking to me in the other shops.

"I'm actually wondering if you have anything for humans?"

Both the shop attendants then look at Ensley and smile broadly. They pet her and then look back at me, "Of course, but you know humans can't have anything delicate. They will break it."

The jewelry shop assistants enthusiastically lead me back to the end of the shop where they have some sturdy silver jewelry.

I point out a short and thick necklace embedded with round green and blue stones. "I'd like to try this one on her."

The shop assistants nod, and one takes out the necklace while I remove Ensley's leash and tell her to stay.

The other shop assistant puts the silver necklace on Ensley, and we all look at her.

Ensley looks around.

I don't know what she is looking for. I take her face between hands to stop her. I'm worried that she is scared and is thinking of running without her leash.

She looks up at me and I smile at her.

I think the necklace looks beautiful, the color of the stones bringing out her green eyes.

Ensley touches the necklace with her fingers and a curious look on her delicate face.

I nod to her. Letting her know she looks beautiful with this on. "Do you have matching bracelets?"

The other shop assistant nods, "We also have anklets and nipple rings in the same design."

One of the shop assistants brings them all out, "I'm not going to pierce her nipples, she isn't an Imperial woman, but I'll take the bracelets, anklets, and the necklace."

"Any earrings?"

It just occurs to me that I don't even know if Ensley has pierced ears. I then look at her ears, and she jumps from my hand, brushing back her hair, which makes my penis stir. I'm surprised to see that not only does she have pierced ears, but she has more than one hole in them.

"Yes, the earrings too then." I caress her pink little ears before pulling my hands away.

Ensley smiles up at me and then looks back down at the bracelets.

I'm pleased that she likes them too.

The sales assistant takes off the necklace to wrap it with the rest of the jewelry. Ensley makes it clear she wants to wear the bracelets, so I allow it.

I put Ensley's leash back on. I realize that she must be hungry and tired now, after all of this. I know that humans tire quickly. "Is there a restaurant on the station that allows pets?" I ask.

"Yes, on the second level. It's called Maliok's. Green sign."

I thank the shop assistants and then proceed to the restaurant. Ensley is so frightened to get in the lift that I have to carry her. I'm beginning to think she's simply afraid of everything new. Thankfully, once we are on the second level, she is fine to walk again. I see many human pets with their Imperial masters on this level and I easily find the restaurant.

Ensley has to sit at my feet, but the floor doesn't look too dirty. I have already decided that she would have another shower when we return anyway, so I sit down at the table and point to the floor. Ensley frowns but sits at my feet. Every time I look down at her, she looks a bit sad. I caress her head and tell her she is a good human. I regret not having taken some chocolates so I could give her some now.

After we eat, we walk around the station. It's not a large station so it's not surprising that I meet some of my officers, and we go to have a drink in a bar. I take Ensley in, and again she sits at my feet.

I'm pleased to see that she is patient and does as she is told. I think, *After her shower, I'll definitely reward her.*

CHAPTER 4

nsley

SEB PICKS me up and carries me off of the ship. I'm worried he is going to sell me. I'm not walking to my next sale. I don't know what I've done to displease him or maybe it's just my physical health in general he feels isn't up to par, but I want to stay with him. Since I can't tell him with words, I'm doing the best I can with body language. Unfortunately, I'm not winning at this as he's so strong he just picked me up instead of trying to understand me.

As I peek out from his chest, it looks like we are in some kind of alien shopping mall or airport. Then I think, *Come on Ensley, don't be so stupid, it's a space port.* I've never seen so many different kinds of aliens in all my life. I see some of the evil teddy bear guys and some of the green guys who originally abducted me as well as lots of other beings that look like everything from walking goats to white angels surrounded by mist. All of these aliens scare me. I'm glad that Seb is holding me against him, and I'm impressed that he doesn't seem intimidated by the sight of these aliens at all. After walking for about ten minutes, through the busy shopping center, I begin to see more and more grey humans like Seb, and I start to relax a little. I hope that if he is going to sell me, it will be to someone of his race. Another grey human.

After a few more minutes of walking and then back tracking and looking around in the busy port, we enter a clothing store and it doesn't take me long to figure out that it is specifically for humans. I can't believe this exists. I see all kinds of clothes mainly for women and made of space-looking-like materials. It's seriously where Barbarella would shop if she had ever really existed. I'm excited as well when I spot some other humans.

The first human I encounter only speaks Spanish and no English. She's older and is kind of mean so I don't mind that I can't talk to her. She doesn't even condescend to speak a word of English to me, just tells me, 'No hablo ingles.'

Thankfully, Seb doesn't speak to her master for long. As we walk further into the shop, and I see that there is an indoor area for humans to chill without the grey people. I hope that Seb is going to let me go into the area without him. I want to know everything about what's going on, and I figure these humans must know something. I hope this is only a clothing shop with a play area and not somewhere where Seb can leave me for sale, like a puppy in a pet shop window.

I look up at Seb with what I hope are pleading eyes and he takes off my leash and allows me in the area for humans. I'm so happy, but I hide my smile because I don't want to look like an idiot in front of these strangers. I enter the enclosure, and no one looks up. I approach a group of women chatting in Spanish. I ask them if any of them speaks English, and they all reply 'no' and shoo me away. Another group of Spanish speaking women do exactly the same as the first. I try not to cry. I have only a few words in Spanish and none of them useful. I wish I would have studied Spanish in school, but I stupidly studied French because one day I wanted to go to Paris and meet a good-looking French man. *I was such an idiot,* I think. *My mother told me that Spanish would be more useful and who knew that advice even extended to the galaxy.*

A young man approaches me, he looks Hispanic, so I expect to be disappointed that he doesn't speak English. I'm trying not to cry so I'm sure my face expression is anything but inviting.

"Hello," he says. "I heard you. I'm Pablo. I speak a little English."

"Hi, I'm Ensley," I smile, I'm relieved to talk to someone.

"Would you like to kick the ball with me?"

"Are you serious?"

He nods, "Your master is watching us, and I think he's very concerned about you being so close to a human male. If we just talk, he might remove you."

I glance back at Seb, and sure enough, he's standing at the glass looking like an overprotective father. I find this comforting that he's concerned about me and it makes me think he is probably not here to sell me. Or if he is, he's still deciding whether or not to keep me so I want to be the best human I can be for him, "Okay, let's kick the ball, Pablo."

"How long have you been a pet?" Pablo asks me.

"I think about two weeks, but that guy bought me only a few days ago."

"And before?"

"I was with some green guys…"

"Oh, 'the recruiters'," he interrupts me. "That's what we call them."

"How long have you been a pet?" I ask.

"I think about five years. I've lost track. They took me by accident. I was dressed as a woman."

"Oh," I say, surprised. "Are you allowed to dress as a woman now?"

Pablo smiled, "Sometimes. I've a very kind master."

"Is your master grey like mine?"

"Yes, they are part of the Empire. They're called Imperial citizens. I don't know much more than that. I've never been to any of their homeworlds."

"I thought my master was human with grey paint on at first," I admit.

"Yes, they are like us in almost every way. You know humans and Imperial citizens can have children together?"

"I didn't know," I say and look at the ball, thinking about that and now speculating what Seb has in mind for me if he keeps me. I wonder if the doctor told him I can't have children or something and that's why he's going to get rid of me. "Have you been forced to have sex with your master?" I can't help but ask the question.

"I wouldn't say forced," Pablo replies with a broad smile.

"But you do have sex with your master?" I clarify.

"Of course, I do," answers Pablo. "Hasn't your master…"

"No, he's been the perfect gentlemen," I say, glancing back at Seb, but he is gone now.

"Maybe he just wants you to show off. It's expensive to have a human pet. Or you are for the crew. He's military, you know?"

"Yes, I kind of figured that out. Is the Imperial military strong? Should I be worried about his ship being destroyed in a space war?"

Pablo laughed at me, "No, they are the strongest, and no one is at war as far as I know. My master is also in the military."

"And have you had sex with the crew?"

"Some of them sometimes."

"By force," I can't help but ask again.

"You are a little prudish. Are you American?"

I kick the ball back at him, hard, "Yes, and there's nothing wrong with not wanting to have sex or gangbangs with aliens, no matter how attractive they might be."

He picks up the ball and bounces it on his knee, "You'll have to learn how to play the games here Ensley or else your life will be miserable."

"Do you know of anyone who has ever gone back to Earth, been returned? Is it possible?"

"The only way back is death."

I want to reply, but then I hear Seb's deep voice call my name. "Thank you for talking to me."

"You mean, playing with you," he gives me a wink and a smile. "Good luck little American girl."

I nod and go to Seb's side. He attaches my leash and leads me back into the store. He has some clothing for me to try on. I'm relieved to be led into the changing rooms. I'm sure he's not selling me now; he just wants to dress me. *I am a beloved pet*, I think smugly.

However, the Barbarella clothing he wants me to wear is something a space sex worker would wear on the job. It's tight and has lots of leather and shows off my figure. The worst part about most of the clothing is that all the pants are crotchless so that my vulva and my rear up to my tramp stamp are entirely exposed.

The shop assistant's human speaks a little bit of English and tries to explain to me that Seb is going to use me as a sex slave for himself and the rest of his crew and that is why he wants to buy these clothes for me.

I look up at Seb in the reflection in the mirror, and think, *No, there's no way he's going to use me as a sex slave. He seems so nice.*

But when I put my hands over my exposed crotch, he slaps them away, and I think it's ridiculous he wants me to wear this. I try to tell him, through translation with the other human, that it's sexier to cover my sex and leave my midriff exposed, but I doubt she tells him this. So when he slaps my hands away again, I just smile at him because if I don't smile and try to make light of this, even if it is only for myself, I will cry. And I worry, if I begin crying over this situation, I may never stop.

The shop assistant fits the clothes perfectly to me, and all the clothing is both crotchless and without covering for my underarms. I look at myself and think I look ridiculous. Out of all the places that I would want my body covered it's those areas, where the hair is growing back.

I look at the shop assistant's human and ask, "Why don't you have to wear things like this?"

"Oh I do sometimes. They think the most adorable thing about humans is the hair we have on our bodies. Imperial people are entirely hairless except for their heads."

"I don't know much about evolution, but how's that possible?"

She shrugs, "Do I look like Charles Darwin?"

She says 'Charles Darwin' with such a heavy accent it takes me a few tries to get it and then the joke isn't funny. "Are you forced to have sex with anyone?"

"No, I'm a sales dog, as you see."

"And you think I'm for sex?"

"Yes, you're on a military ship. They are all going to have sex with you. I'm surprised he's even buying you clothing."

I look at Seb again in the reflection of the mirror.

He looks back at me, his face unreadable.

I continue staring at him, thinking about everything he's done in the last two days. Nothing leads me to believe he's going to share me with the crew, but then I look at my body with these crotchless pants and think, *But then why is he dressing me like a whore?*

I want to cry, but I try to regain control by thinking about something else. I think about the other women I was with in the cage and decide that if I'm going to be a whore, at least it's with nice smelling grey human-like men. Pablo's words come back to me, 'You'll have to learn how to play the games here Ensley or else your life will be miserable.' I suppress a shudder and my imagination runs wild with terrible gangbangs I'll have to endure.

I'm exited when I can get back into my other clothing that covers both my underarms and crotch. Then we pay, I think.

I don't know how Seb pays for things. I can't see any money or anything exchanged, and I imagine it must be so high-tech, it just happens.

Seb leads me to another shop. I know this shop is supposed to be for humans too, but I can't figure out what kind of shop it is. There isn't much on the shelves, and there's a lot of alien writing. Suddenly, an older woman approaches us with a grey alien like Seb.

I light up like a firecracker when the woman greets me in English.

"Are you from England?" I ask naively.

"Scotland, but that was a long time ago. Where are you from? America?"

"Yes," I want to say Manhattan, but I don't think it matters at this point. "How long have you been here?"

"On this station in this job, only a couple of years. Before that, I was with my mistress in a shop on another station, but I've been away from Earth for most of my life. I was picked up when I was about the same age as you are now, the early twenties, right?" she asks.

"Yes. And have you ever known anyone to escape?"

"How long have you been with your master?"

"Two days."

"Ha. I see. Let me disappoint you right now then, there is no escape. But don't worry, these Imperial people aren't too bad. I mean, they have some extraordinary ideas about humans and don't let your master ever take you to a human pet expert, but other than that, I think you will get along just fine. The galaxy is an exciting place to be and you'll see things very few other humans will ever see."

I cut right to the point because I don't know how much time I'll have to talk to this woman, "I'm worried he is going to rape me. That he is going to let his crew rape me."

"I can ease your mind there; Imperial people never rape. They consider the loss of control, whether it be their emotions or physical, to be the ultimate weakness. In their culture, people who rape are put to death. Imperial people who are overweight are cruelly punished. I promise you he and his crew will never rape you."

"But the woman in the other store told me he was going to use me as a sex slave…"

"Oh well, he will probably want to have sex with you and the other men on their ship too, but don't worry, they will make you want it so bad by the time it happens it won't be rape."

I blush and then frown, "But if I don't want it to begin with, it's still rape. I can't help what my body wants, and it doesn't always agree with my mind."

The Scottish woman frowns thinking about what I said, "I would suggest you not think so much about it. You're his now. What your mind wants," she touches my head condescendingly, "isn't important now. Just follow your body and you'll be fine." She clears her throat changing the subject, "This is the human food store. The recruiters who abducted you also steal food from Earth to sell to pet owners at exorbitant prices. I suggest you buy as much as you can as Imperial food is bland and terrible."

As we walk through the shop, she identifies things for me and reassures me that she has rarely come across a human who has been poorly treated by their Imperial masters. She tells me that I'll be a beloved pet. That I'll want for nothing and all I need to do in exchange is be loyal to my master.

She also informs me of Earth's status in the galaxy and that only pirates and smugglers go to Earth as it's in a cordoned-off area by a galactic UN of sorts.

I'm devastated to hear that. I stop walking, and everyone else stops too. "Do those pirates only give humans a one-way ride out and never back in?"

The Scottish woman gives me a sympathetic look, "I've never heard of anyone ever getting enough UCs together to get a pirate to take them home. Humans are expensive. Even if you escaped, pirates would only sell you to someone else if you came to them to try to negotiate a ride back to Earth. We aren't free. Humans are owned like pets. Just be grateful they aren't allowed to make us slaves."

I must have looked really sad then because she continued softly.

"I know, I know. It's tough. The best thing you can do for yourself now is to put the blinders on and look forward. Concentrate on the positive things in this new life. You will be very well looked after, and you probably won't even have to dress yourself ever again, your master will look after your every need. But you must not cry. Imperial people see that as a sign of weakness, and your master will feel he needs to tame you from such a strong display of emotions."

"A pet," I say, and my voice almost breaks.

She looks at me with a lot of compassion, "Don't cry. You're going to be fine. You need lots of chocolate. I'll make sure your master walks away with a lifetime supply. And, trust me, you will find peace with this. We all do. Just think of it like this, you'll never work again, you'll be adored, even when you're old like me, and you will have seen things in the galaxy very few other humans will have ever seen."

"But I've no more choices."

"I have come to think of that as a good thing. Come on now, chin up. You don't want to be punished for crying. You can cry quietly at night when your master is sleeping."

I try to get control of my emotions. I don't want to be punished. I don't look at Seb though, I just pretend to look through the food options, but most of it is South American cuisine, which I'm not familiar with and I don't really care about right now.

All the time, the Scottish woman assures me again that I'll have a good life and that my master will treat me well as long as I do what he asks. She encourages me to learn his language as quickly as possible, guaranteeing me it is just like another human language. She also teaches me how to say 'yes' in my master's language. She says if I say 'yes' and then his name, he will be delighted.

I try it out and see that she's right. I know she's also done this to show that I can trust in everything else she's said too. I want to ask her more, I want to know why they look human but with grey skin, but we can't talk any longer as Seb is getting frustrated.

As we leave the shop, the Scottish woman gives me a smile and a wink, and it makes me feel a little better. At least I know more now than I did this morning, and she more than any of the other humans I've met today has given me some sound advice.

After the food store, Seb leads me into what appears to be a jewelry store. I'm thrilled. I love jewelry and I can see that the two grey shop attendants are more than happy to help Seb. I just hope he is buying jewelry for me. We go to the back and I'm trying to be as cute as possible because I like what I see here. I'm so happy when he picks out an exquisite thick silver necklace with blue and green stones in it. I think it must cost a fortune, and I love the weight of it around my neck. If anyone could understand me, I would ask for a mirror to see my reflection. However, I can tell by the way Seb is looking at me that the necklace complements my looks. As I look up at him, I think I wonder if I'll ever really want to have sex with him. He is attractive, especially compared to the other aliens I've seen, but he's still an alien and grey.

I lose my train of thought when he brushes my hair back behind my ears. His touch sends a shiver down my spine. I assume he is checking to see if my ears are pierced. I continue looking up at him, but we don't make eye contact. His face is serious considering the earrings, and I find this look endearing.

I wonder if he is going to ask the jewelers to have my name engraved on the necklace like a dog tag. They are talking back and forth. Then some matching bracelets are put on both of my wrists. I really love the matching bracelets and feel like I've won a small victory when Seb allows me to keep them on as we leave the shop. I assume that the rest is being sent ahead to the ship because we don't have anything else that we have bought. But then I begin to question if we really bought anything as I still haven't seen Seb actually pay for anything. I wish I could ask him.

I find it endearing the way Seb talks to me as we walk. I've no idea what he's saying, but he obviously expects me to be able to be smart enough to begin learning his language which gives me some hope that even though I'm pet I may not be just like a dog. Unfortunately, my thoughts drift to slavery on Earth and I remind myself that slaves could always speak their masters' languages and that didn't insure them any special treatment. I wonder if it would be better that I didn't learn to speak but instead just remained like a puppy who obediently follows him around.

Next, Seb takes me to a restaurant. I must sit on the floor at his feet and eat with my hands. I have to eat strange green noodles that are served cold. They taste like salty vegetables and have a terrible aftertaste. I lick my fingers to get the salt off them, but Seb shakes his head at me. So, I'm forced to sit there on the floor waiting for him with dirty hands. As I sit there, I think, *I'm glad no one I know will ever see me like this.*

After we eat, Seb runs into some other men from his ship as we are walking through the space port, and again I have to sit at his feet while he and his men drink. Sometimes they spill on me or accidentally kick me, and I don't like it, but I don't want to make Seb angry, so I try to sit as close to his feet as possible and hold on to his strong leg.

Finally, we go back to the ship. I'm so tired. All I want to do is sleep, but Seb has other plans. Once we enter his quarters, he strips me and then drags me into the cold shower. I, of course, try to run away because it's so cold, but he keeps a firm grip on me. When I'm clean and shivering, he tucks me into my bed, naked, and tells me what I suppose is, 'go to sleep.' I put the warm blanket over my head for heat and fall asleep almost immediately.

THE NEXT MORNING, I wake up to the young man petting my hair rather than tapping on my nose.

I wonder where Seb is but assume he must have already left for work. I sit up, but I feel so ill, I immediately lie back down again and close my eyes. I feel like I have a fever.

The young man tries to get me to get up a few more times, but I just feel too ill to get up.

I continue to shake my head at him. I even take his hand and put it to my forehead and say in English, "Hot."

He seems to understand this and leaves me alone. A few minutes later Seb comes to me.

I open my eyes when I hear his familiar voice, but I don't sit up.

Seb kneels down next to my bed and touches my cheek with the back of his cool hand, and after some soothing words that I don't understand, he gently picks me up and carries me naked to sickbay.

I'm too ill to protest my state of undress.

Once there, Seb sets me on a cold silver medical bed. He and the same doctor as yesterday begin talking about me. Then Seb puts his hands on me, holding me down.

I want to tell him I'm too ill to do anything, but I don't mind his hand on my shoulder or the idea that I'd still have enough spirit to bolt. I worry that the doctor is going to do something painful to me as I watch him collect some instruments. I instinctively tense up as he moves over me with those tools in hand.

Seb says my name and then some other words I don't understand.

I shut my eyes because I can't move. Seb is holding me too tightly.

However, to my surprise, the doctor is not doing anything painful, not even a shot or a suppository.

I open my eyes and watch the doctor wave a little white machine over me. It makes a funny noise and smells even stranger.

I try to not breathe it in, but the doctor then holds my nose, so obviously, I am supposed to be breathing it in. I close my eyes; the smell and taste are like rotten eggs mixed with cotton candy. It's *disgusting,* and that is the last thought I have before I feel so warm I close my eyes.

I DON'T KNOW how long I was unconscious from the cotton candy smell.

All I know is that every time I wake, I see either the young man or Seb there, helping me drink some water or use the toilet. Finally, after what I assume must have been at least a day, if not more, I'm feeling well enough to use the bathroom myself. I rise and on shaky legs go to the toilet.

I don't know where the young man or Seb is. I don't know what time of day it is because I still haven't figured out how they tell time on the ship or where a clock may be. Looking out the window is no good because it's just never-changing space.

I realize that I'm alone in Seb's quarters for the first time and this gives me some motivational energy.

I use the bathroom and then look at myself in the mirror. Everything in the bathroom must be requested otherwise it just looks like a stone room. I've learned the alien words for toilet and mirror. Using these words makes me feel like a witch casting spells when I'm able to conjure the mirror up from the stone wall. So the first thing I always see, is my face smiling wickedly when the mirror appears.

After I mentally congratulate myself again on my superior witch-craft in the alien language to pee and look at my reflection, I search my face for any sign of my illness, but to be honest, I don't think I've ever looked better in my life. My skin is practically glowing, and my eyes have never been so bright. When I'm satisfied that I've not got smallpox or galactic plague scars, I dismiss the mirror, feeling witchy powerful again. In my mind I go over the ten words I now know in Seb's language and remind myself I am getting somewhere.

When I walk out of the bathroom, I check that I'm still alone. I call out for the young man or Seb, but no one answers. I smile. Now is the time I can search the room for anything that might be of interest to me, evidence of another pet before me, other humans onboard the ship, or against all the odds, a way back home.

First, I survey the rooms. There's a bedroom, a sitting area with a desk and a small dining room and of course, a bathroom. I begin in the bedroom. I go through Seb's wardrobe first. I open it, expecting to find something exciting, but I only find my clothes, his uniforms, some shoes and boxes of jewelry. I want to look through all the jewelry, but I figure I'll save that for later. Of the few pieces I see, they are intricate and exquisite I wonder if Seb is a rich man, but then I remind myself that a cavewoman would think my cheap clothing and jewelry was nice. I put the jewelry back and close the wardrobe.

Next, I search his desk. I manage to access the 3D computer that hovers above it, but I don't know how to work it, and it's all in an alien language. I try speaking to it, but nothing happens when I speak English, and my few words of the Imperial language are almost useless. I use the Imperial word, 'yes,' and manage to get through to a lot of screens, but I've no idea what anything is because I can't read. I ask the computer to speak to me by saying "say", but that's obviously not the right word for verbal explanations. Not as if I could understand the answers anyway. It's a waste of time. I give up and use the same words I know for the mirror to turn off the computer.

Then, I merely pass through the small dining room. I eat there every day. I know there's nothing there. Just a table and chairs with a jug of water and three cups.

Finally, I go into the bedroom. I check Seb's bedside tables and under the bed, but there's nothing. I can't believe his quarters are devoid of anything personal. Then it occurs to me that it's probably all on his computer. That he would have no need for real things as it is all there, and I'm a little sad thinking, *I really am as dumb as a dog. I can't read to find anything to help me.* And then my thoughts go even darker, *I'll never have the skills to be anything more than a pet.*

I return to my bed and begin to cry for my future. A future that I know I can't change. I let myself go with the stark realization of what being a pet really means. I'll never be anyone important to anyone except for Seb, as his pet. It's heartbreaking to fully comprehend this, and I know somewhere even though I knew I was a pet, it wasn't until this moment that I really understood, so I let myself cry. I have always found that hitting rock bottom, allowing myself some moments of self-pity, is sometimes the only way to push myself back up.

I ugly cry for about an hour.

When the young man returns. I continue to cry. He comes over and pats my head and tries to calm me with the sound the Imperial people make when they think they are soothing, a "Zzzz" kind of sound.

I don't acknowledge him even though I do like that he is comforting me. It makes me feel better, even though I'm a pet.

Soon, Seb enters and comes directly to me. He picks me up. He holds my naked body against his clothed uniform and talks to me sweetly.

I begin to calm myself and think, *But I can't deny, I like being Seb's pet.*

* * *

Seb

I FEEL guilty that Ensley became ill from something she picked up on Fuloir station. Without a doubt she caught something from one of the other humans in the play area.

I'm glad that we are not going to be close to any more stations for a while. I don't want to risk her health again. My doctor scolded me for taking a human fresh from Earth onto such a busy station. I reminded him that we had paid a visit to sickbay prior to entering the station and he hadn't said anything then. My doctor made an excuse which caused me to smile, just as I had hoped, everyone is already just as charmed with the human Ensley as I am.

After three days of resting, she's completely recovered, but she must have been traumatized by her illness because today, when I returned to my quarters, she was crying over it. I comfort her, of course, but all the while thinking, *Humans really are unable to control their emotions.* And I wonder if I'll have the strength to discipline her out of these bad habits.

While I comfort my pet, I dismiss my squire. When she has finally calmed herself, I go to the wardrobe and pull out some of her clothing and ask, "Do you want to go for a short walk around the ship?" I think it'll be good for her to get some exercise and I know that the crew would like to see that she is better.

I repeat my question a couple times. After the fourth time of asking the question with some hand gestures, she understands and agrees.

She says, "Yes, Seb."

As usual, I'm charmed by hearing her speak Imperial and I smile as I dress her.

Once dressed, I slowly walk her around the ship with her leash. As we pass some of my officers on our walk, they stop to pet her and compliment her appearance.

Ensley uses her few words of Imperial with the men and I'm pleased that they are as enchanted as I am by her. We are a beta class ship and therefore are sent on longer missions than most. These missions can be monotonous, so I hope to elevate some of the boredom with the introduction of Ensley.

I look down at her adorable face as she watches the men and hope that she will come to enjoy their company as much as they will do hers.

WEEKS PASS, and Ensley begins speaking Imperial more with each new day. She asks me simple questions like, "What are you? What am I?

Who is that?" and I try to answer her simply so that she can understand.

Today she is at my feet while I work at my desk in my quarters, and when she asks again about our location, I expand the 3D map of the galaxy and show her my ship on it. I don't think she will understand, but I figure she might like looking at all the colors. I know very well that she likes colors. When we go on walks, she enjoys looking out the windows at passing nebulas and planets.

"Look, Ensley, this is our ship here," I point to the little red dot. I expect her to ask why it's red, but she doesn't.

"Where is Ensley's home?"

I feel sorry for her. She is so ignorant she can't even find her solar system on a map of our galaxy. I point to her solar system, "It's here, on the edge, near Trappist territory."

"Who are the Trappists?"

I try in vain to explain the Trappists as humanity's nearest neighbors, but she doesn't have the vocabulary to understand. As she often does when she doesn't want to talk anymore, she just shakes her head until I stop talking. I pat her on the head, giving up.

Then she sits at my feet quietly. I find that I enjoy having her with me, always touching me in some way when I'm in my quarters. She is warm and soft.

A FEW DAYS LATER, I bring up the 3D map of the galaxy on my computer again and ask Ensley where we are. I have some chocolate for her if she can correctly find the red dot.

She gets up on her knees and looks at the map, then she looks at me.

Her eyes focus on the chocolate. She stands, looks at the map and points to the red dot.

I smile, "Well done, clever human." Then I give her the chocolate.

Ensley sits back down and happily eats her prize.

Just for fun, I ask her, "Ensley, where is your home?"

I don't expect her to remember, but I can't help myself I'm curious.

Human pet experts say humans can only remember things for a day or two and then they forget, everything else for them is based on instinct or imprint from their training.

Ensley puts the rest of her chocolate in her mouth and looks at my empty hands. "Chocolate?"

"I'll give you another treat if you can show me where your home is."

She stands and looks at the map again. This task to find her solar system is made trickier as the map is in a slightly different position than it was a few days ago. She walks around it a couple times. I can tell she is really thinking about it because her face is quite serious. After a minute, she points to an area of the map, which is almost correct.

I enhance that area of the map to make it larger and ask her, "Are you sure?"

She shakes her head and then correctly identifies her solar system excitedly, "Ensley's home," she says.

"Well done, Ensley. I will get you another chocolate." As I walk to my dining room, I can't help but be impressed with her memory. *Maybe this is just a one-off*, I think.

I return and give her another treat, and she is thrilled with this. After she eats it, she wants to rest her head in my lap while I sit at my desk. I both love and hate when she does this. I love to have her so close, and her human smell is so pleasing, but at the same time, it makes me aroused having her face so close to my groin. I assume it's her barbaric nature that makes her want to put her head there.

WE HAVE DEVELOPED a nice routine now, and I feel that Ensley is ready to begin fulfilling more of her duties as a pet onboard. In the morning, I specifically stay late to put her in her real human-pet clothing myself, which she has not worn since I bought them on Fuloir station.

I expect Ensley to want to wear these clothes as they show off all her beautiful fur that has grown back nicely covering her sex. I cannot help but pet it and run my fingers through it as I dress and undress her.

Ensley looks at the clothing and shakes her head.

I ignore her and put on the clothing. I bring up a full-length mirror so that she can see herself. I'm pleased with the way that she looks. She has on a form-fitting metallic silver shirt that covers everything except her arms with fitted black trousers that cover everything but her vulva and rear. She looks adorable.

Ensley shakes her head again and puts her hands over her vulva. Our eyes lock in the reflection of the mirror, "Don't Seb."

I take her hands away with one of my own and hold them away. Then I pet her vulva with the other. "You need to be proud of your body. It's beautiful. Humans are lovely."

Ensley looks up at me, pleadingly, "Not beautiful to me."

"You look as you should. Now let's go for a walk." I put on her leash and lead her out around the ship. Usually, she holds her head high and is pleased to see some of the familiar faces of the crew, but today she is just looking at her feet. "Head up, Ensley," I remind her. I'm very proud of her appearance, she is a good-looking human with fur in all the right places. I know my men will love to pet her, and I think she will like it too. Humans are known to love attention, especially any kind of sexual attention. As with everything with Ensley, I know she is shy with anything new, but once she becomes accustomed to it, she will begin to appreciate it.

When Ensley refuses to hold her head up, I take out a little whip made especially for human-pets and smack her rear with it, causing her to jump. This is the first time I've ever intentionally hurt Ensley and I hope that she learns quickly. I don't like having to strike her, she's small and harmless. I remind myself that her settling-in period is now over.

Some of my officers see us walking towards them and smile. They immediately begin stroking Ensley's fur on her vulva and under her arms.

Ensley pulls against her leash and tries to move away from their hands.

71

I tell her firmly, "Let them stroke you. No one is going to hurt you." I don't understand why she doesn't want this attention. I know it must feel good for her to be stroked. I say to my men, "You know Ensley, this is new for her and everything new scares her. Be gentle."

My men begin speaking to her sweetly as they touch her.

When she still resists, I take the human-pet whip and use it on her vulva.

She jumps and looks up at me with a defiant look on her face.

I stun her again in the same place.

Ensley looks at the floor.

I look at my officers and nod.

They begin stroking her again, all the while giving her compliments on her body.

Ensley doesn't resist.

I take a deep breath. I've trained countless men, I've fostered three squires from boyhood into officers, but never have I felt such pity as I do for Ensley when I stun her.

As we walk through the ship, we repeat this same scenario several times, and I can't help but wonder how long it will take for Ensley to become comfortable. I wish I would have just made her wear this clothing from the beginning, but it was my own pride that didn't allow it. I didn't want people to see her lack of hair where human should have hair.

When we return to my quarters, I take off her leash, feed her, and then take off her clothes and put her into her bed for her nap. I look over at her bed, she has the black blankets pulled up all the way over her head, as she likes to do, but I see some movement that is unusual. I walk back over to her bed and pull the blanket back. I notice she is masturbating by rubbing her hand over her clitoris.

She looks up at me surprised.

I slap her hands, "No, Ensley." I must teach her to control herself and understand that I will allow her sexual release at timely intervals.

When I walk off, and she thinks I can't see her, I see the blanket moving again. I again return to her bed and say, "No, Ensley. You cannot do that now."

When it happens a third time, I walk back to her bed, and she tries to move my hand down to her fur, which is wet with her need. I shake my head and return with handcuffs. "I thought I would never have to do this," I say regretfully and handcuff her hands above her head. "Now sleep. It's nap time."

Ensley tosses and turns. I know it must be difficult for her, but she needs to learn restraint. Humans need to be taught this because without it, according to the experts, they will just have sex with anyone, and everything given the opportunity. I must admit, though, the smell of her natural lubrication between her legs is enticing, even more so by the way the strong scent hangs around her, no doubt due to her fur. All the men we ran into today on her walk noticed it and admired her smell. Now, it makes perfect sense to me why humans never evolved as other civilizations. With the fur, the scent of sex is always in the air, so for humans, sex is always the end goal for everything, even their technology is driven by sex.

By the next evening, I myself am so sexually frustrated with the smell of Ensley's desire in my bedroom that I call a woman who sells sex to my room to relieve me.

The muscular grey Imperial woman enters my bedroom and takes one look at Ensley and just wants to play with her.

"Oh, your human is so adorable! Look at her fur and her yellow hair. Can she play with us?"

"Not yet."

"May I pet her?"

"Yes but be gentle."

The woman moves closer to Ensley, who is naked on her bed, curiously looking over at us.

"It's okay, I won't hurt you." The woman says as she begins caressing Ensley's vulva.

I watch and am shocked that Ensley spreads her legs apart and encourages the woman to do more.

I bring out my human-pet whip and use it directly inside Ensley's labia that she is exposing to the Imperial woman.

Ensley yelps in pain and curls up on her bed.

"No Ensley. Control yourself."

I look back at the woman and apologize, "She's still being trained."

"It's okay," the woman says, licking some of Ensley's wetness from her fingers, "She smells good. I understand." Then the Imperial woman comes to me and puts those fingers under my nose. "This is what is driving you crazy. You want to rut with your little pet, but she's not ready yet." The woman's voice is sultry, and her words make me hard.

"Yes, so I need you to do your job."

The woman wastes no time and begins undressing me and licking me all over my body.

"Do you want it as you imagine your pet might want you to take her?"

"I don't know," I answer honestly. I haven't fantasized about what sex with Ensley would be like in detail. What her fur would feel like next to my smooth skin or what it would feel like entering her hot wet human folds.

The Imperial woman turns me around and begins licking my anus. "I bet she would start here first." Her hands spread my butt cheeks apart, and I gasp as her tongue enters me. "Humans are so dirty." She speaks in between licks and flicks of her tongue making me gasp, "I'm sure they lick each other from top to bottom to begin with."

I love the feel of her warm tongue. I suck in my breath before answering, "I don't know. I have only seen a few videos of humans having sex."

"And?" she looked up at me.

I put my hand on her head and directed her back to my anus, "They didn't seem to do much mouth play at all."

"Or perhaps," she turns me around and begins licking my testicles. "What about this? I hear humans like to play with balls."

"She does like to play with balls," I say, remembering her in the human play area. Thinking, *I should buy her a ball.* I could use the printing system to make her one. I smile thinking I will definitely make her a colorful ball. I instinctually look at Ensley then, and she is masturbating again. I push the woman back gently. Reluctantly, I go to Ensley and say firmly, "No. Ensley." To my surprise, she tries to take my penis in her mouth, and I back away and yell at her louder, "No, Ensley. Control yourself."

I have no choice now but to put her handcuffs on and attach them to her bed so she can't touch herself. I turn away from her, but I hear her call me.

"Seb, please."

"No Ensley," I reply sternly not looking back at her. I return to the woman who is waiting for me beside the bed, "Continue."

"Where were we? Oh yes, human pets and balls. Come here, Captain, let me lick your balls like a human. I bet she is fantastic with her sloppy tongue."

The woman draws me closer while she expertly licks my testicles with her wet tongue. I look over at Ensley, and she is trying to turn to rub her body against her bed while she watches us. I wonder, *Is my Ensley untrainable in controlling her sexual desires?* But then I turn my attention back to the woman who is now kissing my lower abdomen, stomach, chest, nipples, and coming up to my mouth. I begin taking off her clothing, massaging her athletic, almost non-existent breasts, nothing like my Ensley and playfully playing with her nipple piercings. Then I drop down to my knees, to her wet hairless sex, and begin kissing all around her vulva and inner thighs. "My little human pet made you wet too," I comment. "Do you want to lick all of her sweet drenched fur as well?"

"She smells so sweet, what can I say? I want to pleasure her and be pleasured by her. I want to feel her hot alien tongue on me too."

"Now you are building my fantasies," I say while beginning to take long licks up her labia, stopping just before I reach her clitoris. One of my great pleasures in life was having sex with women who orgasmed while my penis was inside of them and one of the only ways to be sure that happened, was to make them orgasm at least once if not twice before actual sex. Now, I was familiar with the woman I was with now and knew that she would come easily after one orgasm, but it didn't mean I was going to rush her. As my tongue caresses her Imperial desire, I say, "But humans are complicated and must be trained first, or else they can be ruined, either wanting to have sex with everyone and everything or wanting no one."

The woman puts her hands in my hair trying to guide me, "I'd say she is fortunate in having you for a master. She will love the way your tongue slides across her. I was so happy when you called for me. I've missed your tongue, Captain."

After a few minutes, when I know I have her in the final moments before orgasm, she pulls my hair, making some strands come loose from the braid I always wear. I'm somewhat annoyed that she is trying to hurry me.

"Yes, Captain. Right there. Gods, use your teeth. Yes."

I don't disappoint her. I put one finger inside of her vagina and slowly pulled it in and out, "And my fingers? You want those too?"

"Yes, your fingers."

"And then me?"

"Especially your penis." Then the woman says breathlessly, "and your pet will worship your large penis just like I do."

I begin moving my fingers faster, bringing the woman to climax, and then I flip her over and pound into her. Holding her hands back behind her, just as I will do to Ensley the first time, I take her. As I move in and out, I use the other hand to pull the woman's hair back with just enough force to bring her pleasure. I can feel her body tensing up again, preparing to orgasm again from this new position.

I can't help but look over at Ensley while I'm thrusting. She is moving against her bed with her body intently watching us.

Our eyes met and hold while I make the Imperial woman come again. She is moaning and I see Ensley open her mouth at the same time. I realize that this must be torture for Ensley to watch given humans' sexual nature, but I think it's good for her to know her place.

I look back to the Imperial woman and roll her over onto her back. I lift her hips and her ankles are on either side of my neck. I thrust into her hard until she is coming again and then I do too.

When I'm finished I lie next to the Imperial woman. I run a hand down her sweaty body stopping to gently play with her swollen clitoris.

She jumps at my touch.

"In my next life, I want to be a woman," I say absently.

The woman laughs, "Why?"

"Because there is no question as to which sex enjoys sex more. Women can come and come and come. It must feel amazing."

"Well," she says moving my hand away, "we can orgasm again and again, but only with other people who know what they are doing. Women can also have the worst sex too, sometimes we have sex with men without ever orgasming. I would say, it's better to be a man, even if you only orgasm once each time."

Now it's my turn to laugh, "Maybe, but I've seen women almost pass out from the pleasure. I can't even imagine what that would feel like, but I want to." I hold up my hand to stop her from interrupting me, "And no it doesn't count with a robot. I mean with a real person."

I look over at Ensley and decide to give her something if she can prove to me she is learning. I walk over to her little bed and undo her handcuffs, "Don't touch yourself." I make some hand gestures to make sure she understands me.

I am sure she does because she just looks at me, annoyed.

I take her hands and lay them on her stomach.

Ensley doesn't move her hands, but to be sure she understands, I show her the human-pet whip.

She replies, "Yes, Seb."

I resist smiling. It still pleases me so much when she says my name.

Then I have a glass of wine with the Imperial woman on my bed as she tells me about recent events in the Empire and of course on the ship. Sleeping with her was not only for sex but for information. During this entire time, I keep one eye on Ensley to make sure she doesn't touch herself.

Throughout the hour, she doesn't. She doesn't even move her hands from where I placed them, and her green eyes don't leave me either.

To reward her, I call for my squire and ask him to bring some chocolate. I know this is Ensley's favorite.

When he arrives with the chocolate, I take the chocolate and dismiss him, "Ensley, look, I have chocolate here."

She looks up at my hand, but not moving.

I can see in her eyes that she wants it, "Because you were a good human, you can have some."

She sits up, and then I give her the chocolate.

"Is that good to encourage such dirty human behavior?" the Imperial woman asks, referring to Ensley trying to masturbate before.

"She hasn't touched herself in the last hour. And I'd say, I know more than you do about training people."

The woman shrugs her shoulders, "She's not a person, she's a pet. She needs your whip more than she needs treats. I can see already you and your men are going to spoil her."

I dismiss the woman after paying her UCs with my fingerprint. Before I get back into my own bed, I go back to Ensley's bed and tuck her in. As I look down at only the top of her head sticking out from under the covers, I say gently, "Go to sleep, Ensley." And I hope I am not too kind to her.

* * *

Ensley

I WAKE up and still have the taste of dark chocolate in my mouth. I love that chocolate. I wonder if this is from South America or Europe or somewhere. One thing is for sure this chocolate wasn't the regular kind I used to buy from my local grocery store.

As usual, the young man is in front of me, stroking my hair to try and coax me out of bed. When I get up, he leads me to the bathroom by holding my wrist as he always does. At first, I thought he did this because he thought I wouldn't remember to go to the toilet, but now I think he does it because he likes to touch me. He's sweet and always gives me what I want so I don't struggle against his cool hand.

After he's made sure I've gone to the bathroom and brushed my teeth, he dresses me. I'm never allowed to dress myself, which in some ways, I really like. It makes me feel like a pampered princess with all these large, grey men looking after me and doing everything for me. However, I can't pretend that this is how it will be forever. I know I will have to pay for this luxury. I look down at my crotchless clothing and know that this is only the beginning of the payment for my relaxed lifestyle. I'm trying to get used to the crew petting my vulva and underarms as I'm paraded around the ship, but it's difficult. I remind myself constantly that this all could have been much worse, thinking about Hillbilly, but even that memory is fading. It's been a long time since I've seen any other aliens, so the fear of them seems like a dream. These grey aliens are my only reality now and I am trying to let go of who I was. Trying not to think too much about wanting more than this.

It goes without saying that after all this touching and condescending sweet talk to me on my walks, I'm sexually frustrated. I'd have sex with a chair if I was given the opportunity. Still, every time I try to get off on anything or simply with my hands, I'm stopped, and if I'm really unlucky, Seb uses his whip on me. I'm honestly beginning to wonder if someone can go insane from lack of sex. At all hours of the day, my vagina is begging for attention. It's all I think about. Anything that looks somewhat phallic, I think about putting it inside me.

The only minor relief I get is from the chocolates Seb gives me as treats. A long time ago, I heard that chocolate releases the same endorphins in the body as sex. I've no choice but to hope that's true given the situation I'm in now.

I don't know where my chocolate is kept. I imagine there must be a kitchen somewhere I've never seen, but all the officers seem to have access to it. I know this because a lot of the men give me chocolate too. When the young man walks me in the mornings, a few of the officers always have chocolate for me if I let them rub my 'fur' as they call it. It usually makes me more aroused, but I still want their touch, both in the hopes that I might at last find release from their attentions and, of course, for the chocolate.

My only exercise is walking around the ship and kicking my

rainbow ball against a wall in Seb's quarters. The rest of the time, I laze around like a cat. I wouldn't mind if I had books to read or movies to watch, but most of the time I am really bored. The best part of my day is when Seb comes home. He talks to me more than the young man and always cuddles me.

Lately, Seb is concerned that I'm putting on weight. He is trying to put me on a diet I think, but unbeknownst to him, the rest of the crew delights in feeding me when they pet me or teach me some new phrases in Imperial. Or if I remember their names.

I think I look good, but I know that Seb is concerned. He and the rest of the crew have bodies that are comparable to statues of Greek gods. I know that Seb exercises at a gym somewhere on the ship twice a day, and Imperial food is purposefully healthy and unappetizing to keep people from getting fat.

I don't care if I get chubby though, I don't really need to look sexually good for anyone. It's clear they all just want to pet me but not have sex with me. So I'm forced to comfort myself with food and chocolate.

I've tried to seduce Seb into having sex with me, but that has only ended with him giving me the whip which counter intuitively made me want him even more.

I don't understand why he doesn't want to have sex with me. As far as I can see, he has all the same parts as a human man, except he's much bigger and grey. I've had constant fantasies about Seb ever since I saw him with the Imperial woman. I'll never forget how erotic he looked thrusting into her from behind. His muscular body perfect, and all his motions measured as if even in his height of passion, he had control over everything.

Just thinking about it now makes me clench my thighs together. I want that. I want my master. I'm going to try and be the best I can and hope that soon he will reward me with more than chocolate.

Today when he enters his quarters, I go over to him and say, "Hello, Seb." Usually, I don't say anything, trying to just look sexy, but now I'm trying something new because it's occurred to me that maybe he doesn't see me as someone he can have sex with because he sees me only as his pet.

Seb is delighted by my greeting, "Good Ensley." He pats my head and then caresses my vulva.

I lean into his hand. He must feel how wet I am. I want to say, 'It's all because I've been thinking about you,' but I don't think this is what he'd want to hear.

Seb doesn't stop touching me, and I think, *Yes, this is finally it. He's going to give me some physical relief.* But just as I'm really starting to enjoy myself, he removes his hand and goes into the sitting-room.

I immediately follow him and sit at his feet. Careful to keep my hands away from my throbbing sex, but there's nothing I want more than to reach down and rub myself frantically. I do the next best thing then, I put my head in his lap, my head facing his crotch. I'm hoping I will drive him as crazy as he is driving me. I purposely even breath heavily, hoping my warm breath will jump start some action. But he only casually caresses my hair as he does his work.

Seb and I don't often have conversations. There are two reasons for this. First, I don't have a great grasp of the language to have in-depth conversations about anything. I'd say that on a good day I have the understanding and vocabulary of a five-year-old. Second, I'm his pet, and my role, as I see it, is to give him unconditional love, and he does the same for me. I'm okay with this. Of course, it's not what I dreamed of when I was a girl, but who can predict being abducted and sold by aliens? Also, it's been months now, and even though I know the location of Earth now, I've no idea how I'd ever get back there. I've wholeheartedly resigned myself to the fact that I'm never going to be able to return and that my life with Seb is the best life I'll ever have. I try not to think about what would happen to me if something were to happen to him. It's something that creeps into my thoughts when I'm all alone kicking my ball and it scares me. I can't read, I can hardly speak, I'm not an Imperial citizen. When my language is good enough to be taken seriously and when I get the courage up to hear the answer, I will ask Seb what would happen to me if something were to happen to him.

When I'm not thinking dire thoughts, I try to just enjoy the closeness of another person. I don't think of the grey men as aliens anymore because as far as I can tell the only difference between them and humans is their skin color. In the evenings, I touch Seb and he touches me and we comfort each other this way. Sometimes we sit on the sofa and he runs his hands through my pubic hair for hours. I find it strange and uncomfortable at times, but it gives him so much peace I let him do it.

I fell asleep with the boredom of breathing heavily on Seb. He wakes me up. I'm fed my dinner, which I can hardly eat tonight because every time I look at Seb's handsome grey face, all I can imagine is his face licking my clit. I'm sure my pupils are enlarged with the wanting of him. My thighs are cliched together, and I move a little on my chair as much as I can in my own wet desire to try to find some relief, but as usual nothing seems to help.

After dinner, I'm surprised that Seb doesn't just take me back into the sitting room to sit at his feet while he continues to work at his desk. Instead, he dresses me in a one-piece outfit that is both crotchless has holes in the shirt part, leaving my breasts completely exposed. In my past life, I would have felt like a whore wearing this, but in the here and now, all I can think is, *Please Seb have sex with me in this outfit.*

When Seb is satisfied with my appearance, he puts on my leash and takes me out.

"I've got a surprise for you," he says as we walk down the familiar hallway.

I've become accustomed to my breasts bouncing everywhere since I haven't been given a bra since I came onboard, but I'm embarrassed now that they are bouncing everywhere for everyone to see as we walk. I put my hands over them to stop them from bouncing.

Then I heard the familiar, "No, Ensley," from Seb.

I put my hands down before he punishes me with his little whip. Not because of the pain but because if he were to use that little whip on my nipples, I might die for the next level of arousal it would take me to.

As we walk through the ship, all the men stop and watch us as we walk by. I'm surprised that Seb doesn't stop for the men to touch me, but we continue walking, and my breasts bounce up and down with the rhythm of my fast steps. I look at the men as we pass, their eyes are on my hard nipples, and I think, *Hmm, just like human men.* And again, I wonder, *Are you really all just a grey version of us? Lost somewhere in the galaxy? Or did we get lost?*

I'm a little disappointed that Seb doesn't stop and allow the men to touch me. I've heard that it's possible for women to come just from men playing with their breasts. The men we pass look so hungry for my breasts, I'm sure only a little bit of tugging and playing with my nipples would bring me to some kind of orgasm.

A wave of wetness coats my thighs just thinking about it. All I want is relief. I look up at Seb, but he doesn't look down at me.

We arrive at another man's quarters. I've been here before and I know he's a friend of Seb's and an officer. We are greeted by five other men inside. His friend comments on my breasts. I assume that's the word he uses because he then caresses one of my nipples between his thumb and forefinger, saying, "Nice."

It feels so good, despite the awkwardness of being so exposed.

I repeat the word "Breast," and all men smile at me.

Then they all surround me, taking turns playing with my nipples. I close my eyes, trying to will my release, but it still seems far off. So much for all those people who said it was possible to orgasm from people just playing with your breasts.

Seb also caresses my nipple. His touch feels better than anyone else's. He speaks to me softly, "Breast. Good, Ensley."

I sit on the floor at Seb's feet. I wrap my arms around his leg and put my cheek against his uniform. I know as the night continues, they will play electronic card games while they drink wine and talk and Seb will take me onto his lap as he always does and caress my hair as he talks. So I don't mind starting out on the floor first.

The men turn on the 3D computer in the middle of the table. This isn't that uncommon, and I'm preparing myself to zone out to some alien thing I can't understand, but to my surprise, it's a video about humans. I watch the screen intently, there are lots of humans on leashes with their Imperial owners. Then the video cuts to a section directed at me, from one human-pet to another. Unfortunately, it's in Spanish, and I don't understand.

I look up at Seb, "I can't understand."

Seb sighs, "It's okay." Then he pauses the video, "You will..."

I don't understand the rest of what he says. I don't have the vocabulary. I focus on the paused video and wonder why it was just a woman speaking in Spanish with no pictures or diagrams. There's nothing more I want to do than to please Seb, in the hopes that he would desire me the way that I want him to.

Unfortunately, when the men realize that I can't understand the video, they turn it off, and it seems like I'm completely forgotten, and it turns into just a regular night of Seb and his friends hanging out. I'm momentarily crestfallen that somehow, I've done something wrong by not being able to understand the Spanish or the alien language enough to know what they want from me. I want to tell Seb, 'I'm sorry,' but I know better than to interrupt him now, so I just sit on the floor, wondering if the surprise he mentioned earlier is also canceled. So much time passes I question if I misheard him earlier when he used the word 'surprise.'

Soon more officers come in, and they all began talking and drinking wine. As the night goes on, Seb allows a lot of the men to pet me and play with my breasts. Never enough to do anything more than drive me crazy with sexual frustration, though. I honestly think I'm going to die from sexual frustration now.

My body is aching and I have a constant wetness between my legs. I assume the only reason I don't have a yeast infection is because I wear crotchless clothing.

Through all the conversation, I hear the man standing in front of me ask Seb, who's across the room, something about me. I don't understand the entire question, but I see Seb stiffen, then Seb looks at me, trying to decide something.

I nod to him. I don't know what I'm agreeing to, but I'm tired of waiting for something to happen. Seb mentioned a surprise and I wanted a surprise.

Seb rises from his seat and comes to stand in front of me.

I'm excited and scared for him to tell me what to do next.

"All of you sit down then," he says to his men. Then he turns to me and says, "Ensley, now you can touch yourself. You have earned it."

I can't believe what I'm hearing. I look to his hand for the small whip, but his hand only holds a cup of wine. I still don't move to touch myself. I'm so sexually frustrated, but I'm also scared of displeasing him. I don't trust my language skills. I worry I want this so much I only hear what I want to hear.

"Ensley, you can masturbate now," Seb repeats himself.

"I can masturbate?" I ask, still unsure. "I can touch?"

"Yes," he takes my hand and brings it to my hairy, wet sex.

I look up at him, and then at all the men quietly watching us. There's nothing I want to do more than to masturbate, but I want to do it privately in the bathroom, in my bed, or just in front of Seb. Not in front of a crowd.

Seb senses my hesitation and puts one of his cool, strong hands on my shoulder, "Ensley. I know you want this. Your little human body is begging for it. We will enjoy watching you bring yourself pleasure. You have earned this." He moves one of his hands to cover my hand and guides it towards my clitoris again.

I look at all the officers, the familiar faces who pet me every day. I don't know why I feel shy. I do want this. I want to come so much.

Seb begins to guide my hand in circular motions.

It isn't long before my natural instincts quickly take over, and he moves away as I am finally getting exactly what I want. I'm rubbing my clit in slow circular motions, trying to draw this out for my own pleasure. My eyes are closed, imagining that I'm alone with Seb. I tell myself that I'm doing this to please him and that after I do this, he will have sex with me, just as he had with the Imperial woman. I imagine him holding me like he held her and thrusting into me with his measured movements.

My fantasy is somewhat broken though when he commands me.

"Open your eyes, Ensley. Look at me when you come. I'm your master."

I open my eyes, and they lock with Seb's grey ones. "I don't know if I can," I say, closing my eyes again.

Seb grabs my hand away from myself, "You'll open your eyes, or I won't allow this."

"Yes," I say, and he lets my hand go. I return it to my throbbing clit and rub. Faster and harder. It feels so good. My whole sex seems to be drenched in wetness, my fingers are almost slipping, but I don't stop rubbing, and I keep my eyes on Seb as he has bid me to do. But then my eyes wander to all the other pairs of eyes on me. They are all watching me hungrily, and I wonder if this is going to turn into a gangbang.

I've noticed that Imperial people have a lot of strange ideas about humans, and I wouldn't put it past them to think that I'd love a gang bang. However, right now, they wouldn't be too wrong. I'm so aroused I would agree to almost anything. I know I'll regret everything tomorrow, but right now, I'm so drunk on lust, I'm willing to do anything to sexually gratify myself

Seb commands me, "Keep rubbing, Ensley."

My eyes hold with Seb's again. He's so dirty, making me do this in front of his crew. But I'm so dirty too because I'm actually beginning to enjoy doing this for him in front of his friends. The only thing that would be more perfect is if he would take off his trousers and have sex with me right here. It isn't long before I bring myself to the hardest climax of my life. The spasms make me crumble to the floor with the force of the orgasm, but even then, I don't take my hand away from my throbbing body because I'm not thoroughly relieved.

Seb knows it too. All the men know it. They have all taunted me for months, petting my vulva and now pinching my nipples.

"Continue, Ensley," Seb commands.

I begin to rub myself frantically, and I reach that point where my clit is numb and tingly, and every touch feels too good. I'm paralyzed with the pleasure of it. There's nothing but me and my fingers in the world. My touch has every part of my body still except for my fingers, I never want to move. I come again, multiple little orgasms racing through me.

"Again, Ensley."

"I can't," I say, almost breathlessly looking up at Seb from the floor.

He takes out his little whip and uses it across my butt that is half-turned up. The whip that usually caused only pain now brings pleasure too and I come again from the punishment. I even squirt a little from my urethra, which brings on further delight from the men watching me.

I'm lying with my breasts pressed against the cold floor and my butt up in the air. All I want is for someone to put something inside of me. I want to beg for it, but I know if I ask, I'll never receive it. I know enough about Imperial culture to know that much.

I remain still. Waiting for what will happen next.

I can feel so much wetness running down my legs.

Seb comes over and flips me on my back. He pinches my nipples and says, "Come one more time, Ensley, like this."

I look up at him like he is a Greek god. I want to please him. I think, *Maybe he will really reward me later if I do this.* I lie on my back and begin touching myself again, my own wetness all over my vulva and my upper thighs. After a long time and such an ache, I make myself come so hard from doing what he wants I squirt again, but this time it seems like it goes everywhere. In my past life, I would have been embarrassed by all of this, but right now, I don't care. I just want to please Seb.

My master pats my head, "Good, Ensley."

I feel satisfied and proud.

After I come down from the multiple orgasms high and realize what I've done in front of all of these men, I'm suddenly mortified. All the confidence I had a few seconds ago is gone. I've pleased Seb, but I've also defiled myself. I lay there for a minute on the floor, too ashamed to move.

I hear Seb call the young man in. I'm relieved that the young man was not in the room for my performance. Although Imperial people seem to have some strange traditions about sex, they at least felt that it wasn't something the young men on the ship should be exposed to, at least as far as I could tell.

Nudity on the other hand, for all of them is nothing though. Everyone is nude in the night as no one wears any kind of pajamas and they think nothing of calling on someone naked or praying in the nude, so the young man seeing me nude is nothing to him and probably holds no sexual innuendos. I know if the young man would have watched my performance, it would have been wrong both by Imperial and human standards. I'm relieved for this small grace. That there's someone I see every day that hasn't witnessed a new level of my fall from being a person.

The young man comes and takes me to the bathroom and cleans me up. I can't read his expression, but he does try to shield the other men's eyes from my body with his own as he showers me. However, the other men tell him to do his work to the side so they can enjoy the sight of my body. The men continuously keep commenting on how cute I am and how adorable my face looked when I orgasmed.

These words are mortifying to me. I want to cry but I know they will only see that as a sign of my human barbarism. I tell myself, *They all think this is normal. I must convince myself this is normal. Seb loves me.*

Some of the men start touching me again, and I try to back away from them. I don't want anyone touching me right now.

The young man tells them off, but they don't listen to him.

Seb must have heard my protests because he says something to them, and finally, it's just the young man and me in the bathroom. The young man doesn't seem to care much about touching me in any way, but to get me clean and his familiar methodical hands give me some comfort.

But even still, my thoughts overwhelm me and I begin to cry in the cold shower. *What am I doing here? Is this really my life now? I'm a weird human-pet exhibitionist for grey men?*

The young man ignores my crying. I think he is embarrassed for me. He doesn't put my clothing back as it's disgusting after my performance. He attaches my leash and hands it to Seb, who leads me back to his quarters and puts me to bed with the words, "Don't cry Ensley."

I can't help the tears running down my cheeks. I don't know why, but I want Seb to hold me like a man would hold a woman, not like his pet, but as an equal. I think, *If he holds me like that, then somehow this would all make sense.* But, of course, he doesn't. He just pats me on the head, and then calls for two Imperial women to come to his quarters to have sex with them, while I watch from my bed.

I make eye contact with him as he is in one of the women. I stand on my bed to offer my naked body to him, but he just says, "No, Ensley."

I throw the covers over my head disappointed and just as sexually frustrated as I've been the days before and I wonder again, *Is this really my life? Will I only get to masturbate when he says I can and in front of an audience?* I decide that I will make Seb want me sexually or I will die trying.

THE NEXT MORNING, I wake up, and instead of the young man being there it's Seb, and I think, *It must be a day of rest and I lost count of the days.*

He picks me up, as we are both naked and takes me to the shower. It is cold. I don't think he needs to wash me as the young man thoroughly washed me last night, but I know better than to protest.

Seb washes himself and me at length. He takes great pains to make sure my vagina and anus are very clean, and all I can think is, *Please say you are going to reward me by finally having sex with me today. All-day. Only then can I survive this kind of captivity.* I half wonder if one of his grey alien gods that he prays to daily has taken pity on me and granted me my one desire.

After we are clean, I wait naked in the center of the room for Seb to dress me, but he turns to me and says, "I'm going to exercise you differently today, Ensley. No walk."

I push my thighs together, and my eyes light up, hoping he finally means sex.

Seb stands in front of me, "Do you want me to put my penis in your vagina, my little pet."

"Yes, Seb." It's terrible I know, but I'm turned on that he called me his 'little pet.' I think about the first human laws ever written down. They were directed towards farmers not having sex with their sheep. I smile to myself and think, *But I'm not really an animal, he just likes to pretend I am.* All the time wishing he call me his 'little pet' again.

Seb goes down on his knees, picks me up like I'm nothing and holds me over his face. His strong arms and hands balancing the entrance to my vagina over his mouth while his tongue begins to lick around it and then thrust inside it.

I'm so thrilled, I almost see black from the excitement and pleasure. My heart is pounding. Somewhere I can hear myself moaning with both the satisfaction of his tongue and the pain of his fingers digging into my hips in such a position. Only a few minutes pass and then I'm coming hard all over his face. It feels so good, too good. I hope this isn't all just a dream, but the pain I feel from his fingers reminds me, this is all very real. And I'm happy for the pain for I'll have ten fingerprint bruises on my skin to prove to myself that this happened.

Seb carries me to his large bed, where I have never been allowed before. If I had been a cat, I would be purring. He turns me over on my stomach, props up my knees, and holds my hands back at my wrists with one of his large hands, "Tell me what you want, Ensley."

"I want you to have hard sex with me, master."

"No, Ensley."

Through my lust haze, all I could think is, *'No?' What's 'no'?* I'm ready to lose my mind. We are so close.

Seb lets go of my wrists and moves away from me.

I watch him walk away confused by his actions.

I get off the bed and follow him to his wardrobe while he begins to get dressed.

"What did I say wrong?"

"I'm not a barbarian or an animal. I don't have 'hard sex' with things, and neither do you. It's obvious you are not ready."

"I'm sorry," I say frantically. My grasp on his language is still terrible. I really don't understand how the word 'hard' could be wrong or vulgar in this context, but I also know better than to ask. I look up at Seb and say, "Punish me now, and then I will do better." I prostrate myself on the floor at his feet. I know that begging is also the last thing he wants me to do now, but I can't help it. Begging makes me feel good about trying to make amends and he's already said 'no'.

"This is my fault. It's too soon," he says.

I look up at him in dismay. His strong and perfect grey body, his massive penis ready for sex. I can't believe he isn't going to have sex with me.

After he dresses himself, he pulls me to my feet and dresses me in a silver shirt and the crotchless trousers. Then he takes me for a long and brisk walk. All the men we pass caress my wet pussy where his mouth had been only twenty minutes before. I want to ask Seb to let one of them have sex with me, but I know he'll only be upset by that. On our walk, I begin to ponder the possibilities of going insane from this kind of hot and cold sexual treatment.

Afterward, Seb brings me back for food and my nap. He strips me down and then puts me to bed. But instead of leaving my side, as he usually does, he pulls the covers back and begins caressing my breasts and playing with my nipples. I'm so frustrated, but I don't want to get my hopes up to only have them crushed again, so I just watch his handsome face as he fondles me.

I'm beginning to believe he really wants me to go crazy.

Seb plays with my breasts throughout my entire nap time and at the end, touches the wetness between my thighs. Smearing it all around. I keep trying to instinctively get his fingers inside my vagina by moving my hips towards his fingers, but he holds me down with his other hand.

"You've got to stop this barbaric behavior," he murmurs, "You must learn control. You must tame your inner human barbarian."

I don't understand all of his words, but I understand enough, "I have control."

"Not yet," he says and then suddenly moves away from me. I feel he did this on purpose to teach me a lesson. Well, he certainly did that.

I'll never say 'hard sex' ever again. Next time, if there is a next time, I'll remain a quiet, horny and grateful pet.

I lie on my bed naked. My nipples can't be any pointier or my vagina any wetter. I want to parade myself through the ship like this, hoping someone will take pity on me and take me against a bulkhead. Unfortunately, I know that won't happen. I get myself up and sit naked at Seb's feet while he does his work in the sitting room as if this has been any ordinary day without the drama.

Seb looks down at me at one point, "If you're good human, you'll be rewarded later."

I actually beam at him for that, hoping that he means we'll have sex and not a reward of chocolate. However, I'm disappointed because, after my afternoon walk, I'm given only chocolate and a pat on the head. It crosses my mind to rub the chocolate over my sex to see if that does anything, but I decide against it only because I don't want to make my sheets messy.

That night before we sleep, Seb is reading something in his bed. I want to talk to him. I want to find out what he wants from me, but I'm not confident enough in the language, and I'm afraid to make him even more displeased. At the same time, I also worry that he doesn't know how crazy he is making me and how confused I am. I do think that he really cares for me and wouldn't want me to suffer this way. But when I put myself in his position and think about being a dog owner, I would not take my dog's opinion seriously because the dog doesn't have the intellect to know what's best for him, and I've no doubt this is how Seb feels about me. Even though I'm just a different color than he is, and I can talk, he still sees me as a lesser species and someone that it's his responsibility to tame into a civilized Imperial creature.

I make a promise to myself that I'll continue to try and follow his rules but at the same time keep trying to seduce him. Keep trying to win some power back between us. *I'm a New Yorker, I'm not just a pet,* I think with a smile. My goal now is to get him to lose control and have sex with me. To make me more than his pet, to allow me to sleep in his bed and sit on his sofa.

. . .

MONTHS PASS, and every day is the same as before as if my public masturbation session and Seb eating me out never happened. I began to question myself, *Am I so sexually frustrated that I only dreamed all of that?* I want to ask someone, but I'd feel like an idiot either way, so I just keep it to myself that I think that I'm beginning to lose touch with reality.

Every day I think about Seb. Everything I do, I think about him. I try to please him in every way. Every chance I think I might win a small battle in the war to seduce him, I take it.

Every day when he returns to his quarters, I greet him, and he pets me. Then I follow him around his quarters and sit at his feet while he does his work. If I'm lucky, he lets me nuzzle my face in his crotch. Then he takes me for walks in my crotchless clothes, my vagina dripping as men stroke me and pinch my nipples. In the evenings, he strips me and puts me to bed.

He usually goes to bed at the same time.

Sometimes he calls a prostitute in, and I watch as he has sex with an Imperial woman, wishing it was me.

Tonight, as I lie in my bed unable to sleep, I decide that I can't take this anymore. I worry I'm really going crazy. I decide I must put my plan to seduce Seb on the hold so that I can prove to myself I am not insane.

I sneak out of my little bed, naked. I quietly pass Seb's bed, go through the small hallway and out of Seb's quarters. I turn to make sure he is still sleeping when the door swishes open, thankfully he is. I run out.

I've rarely been out in the ship during the night hours, and the hallway is darker than usual. I can hardly see. I know the ship well though, so I run fast, desperately searching for someone to have sex with me. Unfortunately, I'm quickly caught by the night guards not far from Seb's quarters.

The guards don't even pet me. One of them picks me up and returns me to Seb.

I can see in Seb's eyes that he's angry, but he doesn't raise his voice. He takes me from the guard, retreats into his quarters and then retrieves my handcuffs and puts them on me. I expect him to put me in my bed, but instead, he positions my hands on the empty wall next to the wardrobe and thrusts my legs apart with his hands.

Then he gets out the little whip.

"Ensley, I am so disappointed. Were you out looking for 'hard' sex?" Without saying anything more, he begins to whip my backside and vagina with hot licks.

I grunt with every strike. It hurts so much. Finally, I cry out, "I'm sorry. I just need you. I'm losing me." I don't have the vocabulary to express my fears about my mental condition and it makes me even more frustrated.

"And you left looking for any man to have sex with? Human barbarian. Will you never learn?"

"Yes, I'm sorry, Seb," he continues to whip me. My lower body is on fire.

"You aren't allowed to leave here unescorted. You're a pet and you will be tamed."

After he whips me, I put my head down in shame and begin to cry. I'm so frustrated, overwhelmed, and tired of these games.

All I want from him is sex, and he refuses to give it to me, but at the same time he teases me to the point of insanity. I'm at my limit. I have nothing to lose now. I crawl over to his feet, my hands still bound by the handcuffs, and begin to kiss his strong, hairless feet, "I'm so sorry." I say in his alien language again and again between kisses.

When he doesn't kick me away, I purposely let my breasts touch his ankles and shins while I let my hungry mouth roam up his legs. I've seen enough Imperial prostitutes to know what he likes. But of course, I have something they lack. Something I know he wants from me so as I begin to move up his body, I'm focused on making sure my breasts rub against him all the while my mouth tastes his clean and smooth skin. I'm inspired because as I lick past his penis, I notice that it is fully erect. I kiss all around it and then his hard abdomen. Then I do something I know no alien woman could do as they don't have breasts; I hold my breasts together with my arms, as I'm still bound, and squeeze his penis between them moving up and down. I look up at him innocently while I do it. Hoping he's not going to throw me off and punish me again. After a few seconds, his eyes are filled with so much desire, I know that he won't be able to resist me now.

I'm giving him what only his human pet can provide.

"You are such a barbarian, but I won't stop you today," he says breathlessly not breaking eye contact with me.

For the first time I feel that I'm winning a battle in this war and it encourages me. I move rhythmically, increasing my speed so that he'll come all over my breasts. I want to be strategic about this. Next time, I'll bring him to the point of orgasm, and then I'll get him to have sex with me. Right now, I must take this small victory, despite my own aching need.

I pump my breasts up and down. I look up at him as I do it and I don't even have to pretend that this is the sexiest thing I have done in a very long time. Up and down. My eyes never leave his grey ones. I'm in control of this situation for the first time. I'm further inspired when I feel some moisture from his penis on my right breast and move faster, pushing my breasts together even harder.

A few seconds later, Seb comes all over my breasts like a hot fountain. I let go of my breasts and sit on the floor, looking up at him. I can feel his hot semen running down and off my nipples. I feel like it's proof of a win for me, like a hot metal for getting my alien master to do something I wanted.

Seb looks at me, "Lick that up and then suck me clean, Ensley."

Master, you are filthy sometimes, I think. I do as he says, I lift my breasts to my mouth as much as I can, and then he helps with his fingers, scooping up his come and putting it into my mouth. I know from watching him have sex with Imperial women that they have some bizarre ideas about bodily fluids.

After I finish licking up and swallowing all of his salty and sweet semen. He picks me up and puts me back in my little bed. He tucks me in, "Sleep Ensley," and then he gets back in his bed and goes to sleep.

Hours later, I'm still painfully awake. My backside is on fire from my punishment, and I'm still in need of sex. I look up at him peacefully asleep.

Drunk with my small victory, I decide I'd rather risk another punishment than stay like this, so I get up and creep into Seb's bed. I've only been here for a minute before and my heart is racing at this transgression. I don't even want to think about what he will do to me if this plan doesn't work.

My hands gently find his penis, and I begin stoking it to attention. It isn't long before I turn myself and angle my body so that his penis is aimed at the entrance to my vagina. I'm just about ready to push back into his erect penis when he puts his large hands on my hips and pushes me away.

"No, Ensley," he says without opening his eyes.

"Please," I begin to beg. I turn and rub my breasts against his big muscular chest, and I'm pleased he lets this happen, "Seb," I try to sound more confident, reminding myself he doesn't like begging. "My vagina aches."

"But this isn't the way. Don't let your human desires guide you."

His hands are playing with my nipples as he talks to me, and his penis is still hard resting against my thigh. I know this isn't a lost cause.

"Let me ride you," I ask. "I want to bounce my breasts while your penis impales me." I purposely say that because I know this is something he would have fantasized about. All the Imperial men seem to be obsessed with my breasts and the way they move with gravity.

Seb doesn't answer, so I slowly push him onto his back and quickly mount him. Or rather try to. His penis is so large that it takes some time for me to accommodate myself. That and I've not had a penis or anything in my vagina in months, maybe even a year, I've no idea how much time has passed since I was abducted and sold.

"You're so big," I say as he watches me.

I hold his eyes hoping he won't throw me off, but he seems almost amused. When I've gotten a good portion of his penis snuggly inside of me, he doesn't even change his face expression. I wonder if he feels anything at all, but I don't want to ruin the moment by asking. It feels so good for me. I want nothing more than to close my eyes and savor every moment, but I know enough about his alien culture to know that to close one's eyes when enjoying something with someone else is considered rude. So, against all my instincts, I maintain eye contact with him as I slowly begin to move up and down. It feels so gratifying, and I unabashedly moan with pleasure, licking my lips and grabbing my breasts, kneading them to bring myself even more pleasure.

"Ride me, Ensley. Make yourself come, my little human."

I smile. I don't need encouragement. I begin riding him faster. I let go of my breasts and place my hands on his muscular grey chest to balance myself and to angle myself so that my clit rubs against his smooth hairless body. It feels amazing. I want him to put his hands on my hips, to strengthen my movements, but he doesn't, and I know that's because he feels like he is doing me a favor by allowing me to ride him, so I'm the one performing again, but right now I don't care and I still count this as a huge victory. I want to command him to call me 'little pet' but I don't want to risk him throwing me off.

"Faster Ensley. I want to see you in all your glory. Make yourself orgasm on me."

I obey him and quickly lose myself in the moment. I don't even know if he comes, but when he lifts me off him, his huge penis is still erect, and I realize that he hasn't. He holds me against his cool body and asks, "Are you satisfied now?"

"Yes," it's only half a lie.

Seb pats my head, gets up with me in his arms, and puts me back in my little bed.

My backside still hurts, but at least I'm not as frustrated as I was before. I fall asleep in minutes. I can't be bothered to wonder anymore about these strange alien sexual practices or how he could possibly not orgasm or sleep after that.

I'm only Seb's pet, and his concerns are not my concerns. My concerns are his though, and I think *He has been the best master ever today.*

CHAPTER 5

nsley

THE YOUNG MAN wakes me the next morning as usual.

I'm disappointed that it isn't Seb. I look around, but he's gone, already on duty, of course. I get up and go to the toilet as I always do, with the young man guiding me. Then the young man's voice activates the shower.

I don't feel like a cold shower right now, so I shake my head.

"Ensley, you are dirty. You must shower. You got the Captain's semen all over your breasts."

I ignore him and try to get past him.

"No, Ensley," he says firmly and smacks my butt that's still sore and probably bruised from the night before.

I yelp with pain.

The young man holds me with one hand and smacks me again and again until I get into the freezing shower. Once I'm shivering under the water, he takes the soap from the robotic arms and quickly spreads it over my breasts, vulva, vagina, and anus. He even puts his finger in and out of my anus to make sure I'm clean. As he does this, I'm so shocked, I squirm and lose my balance on the wet and soapy floor.

I think as I'm going down, *Oh my God, I'm going to be one of those losers who dies in the shower.*

The young man sympathetically yells, "Oh no, Ensley," and then ignoring his own clothing, picks me up from the running water and cradles me to him. "Are you okay? I'm just following orders to get you very clean. Poor Ensley."

It's so strange being cradled by a young man, but then I remind myself he thinks of me as a pet.

A strange kind of pet, but a pet, nonetheless.

"Yes," I say.

The young man puts me down on Seb's bed and then eyes me to make sure I'm really okay. When he's satisfied, he dries me off with Seb's sheets, which I feel is defeating the purpose of the shower but I'm not going to say anything. Then he gets some fresh pet clothes from Seb's wardrobe.

As is our routine, he feeds me and then takes me for my usual walk around the ship. Officers and crewmen alike stop to pet me and talk to me sweetly and condescendingly. I'm becoming sexually frustrated again with all this petting and fingers lightly teasing the folds of my labia.

After my walk, I'm put down for my nap. As I drift off to sleep, I wonder if Seb is going to punish me for sneaking into his bed last night. I hope not.

When Seb returns to his quarters in the afternoon, I go to him and beam up at him hoping that if his intention is to punish me, he will abandon it at the sight of my face. I also say, "Hello, Seb."

This pleases him as it always does, and I'm relieved to see that he doesn't look too angry with me. He pats my head, then scoops me up and carries me to the sitting room.

Today he sits with me curled against his chest while he works from the sofa. One of his hands gently caressing the hair on my vulva as he thinks about something. I know my place, so I never ask him what he is thinking about. I just watch him trying to be as cute as possible, because right now there's nothing, I want more than to kiss him and ride him again as I had done the night before. Last night, I managed to push him twice, so I have high hopes that sex is not out of the question tonight if I'm strategic again.

After about 45 minutes, there's someone at the door. I think this is odd, so just like a dog, I jump up to go see who it might be, even though I'm clearly not allowed to open the door.

"It's okay, Ensley. It's just the doctor."

I stand where I am in the middle of the room, and then the doctor comes in. He has a little bag with him. When he enters the room and sees me, he comes over to me directly.

"Hi Ensley," he says as he pats my head and then runs his hand all the way down to my vagina and circles the entrance, pulling on the hair there just for fun. "Always a little wet down there, aren't you?" he asks rhetorically. Then he gets out a small medical device, and his hand goes to my butt cheeks that still hurt, and he begins healing the pain and bruises. "I hope this won't happen again. You need to be a good human. Do you understand? You must be tamed, or you will be put down."

You won't kill me, will you? I question Seb with my eyes.

Seb shakes his head, "Ensley, the doctor is only joking." Then to the doctor, "Come now, don't scare her. Her Imperial language isn't good enough yet to understand sarcasm."

"She's human; she might not never have the ability to ever understand it," the doctor says nonchalantly as he continues to run a medical scanner over me.

"I understand," I say defiantly to the doctor. I look over at Seb to let him know I'm not stupid. I'm rewarded with a small smile. I want to smile back, but I know that'll only convince the doctor that I'm even more stupid.

"Of course, you do," the doctor says condescendingly. Then he says to Seb, "Just very minor bruising. I've healed it." Then he pats my head, "All done, good human."

I realize this means that I should go somewhere, so I go over to my little bed to sit, but just before I sit down, Seb commands me.

"Ensley, come here."

The last thing I want is to be inspected by the doctor anymore, but I obey because I don't want any more punishments either. I stand in front of Seb and the doctor.

Seb looks down at me. "You must stay here until I tell you to go to your bed, not the doctor."

"Yes, Seb," I reply and put my head down, waiting. I look at his clean black boots and think of how many times I've rested my hands on them while sitting at his feet.

Seb absently caresses my head as he continues his conversation with the doctor, "Breeding is possible then?"

"Yes, of course. She's in good health. Much better than when she first arrived. Earth is such a backward place it's ridiculous anyone could ever believe any of the old myths."

"I agree," Seb says, but I can tell by his voice that he doesn't really agree with the doctor, but I don't understand everything that they are discussing. I'm more concerned with the word 'breeding.' *Is Seb going to breed me with another human, and that's why he never has sex with me? Or rather never come inside me?* All I can think about is being made to have sex with some disgusting human man who's spent his whole life in Imperial captivity while an audience watches with enthusiasm. I feel sorry for all the animals at the zoo now. All these thoughts make me instinctively shake my head.

"Ensley stop shaking your head," Seb slaps my vulva somewhat hard, and as much as I want to hate him for it, I can't. I'm so wound up and sexually frustrated all I want is more, and I want him. Not another human pet. I want my master.

The doctor laughs, "It looks like she's more than willing. Maybe I should go unless you want me to watch to make sure everything goes where it is supposed to?"

"I think it's better we start slow. I'm still very protective over her, and I don't want her to get hurt or scared," Seb says as he escorts the doctor to the door. "In a few months, I might be ready to share."

My mind is running wild when I hear those words, *Please say you are going to have sex with me*, I think over and over again as I watch the men walk towards the door. I don't give any currency to the idea that Seb would ever share me and especially not with the horrible doctor.

After the doctor has been shown out, Seb turns back and looks at me, I imagine he does it to make sure I've not moved from the place where I'm supposed to be waiting for him, but when he turns, he has an expression I've never seen before. I don't know what it is. It isn't anger.

I stare back curiously only because I'm trying to figure out his expression. After a few seconds, I decide it doesn't matter because I know what I want, so I try to make my eyes big and inviting.

Seb walks towards me with purpose and picks me up as he usually does, but it feels like he's holding me just a little tighter than usual. Then he puts me on my feet in front of his massive bed. He rubs one finger up and down, playing with the folds of my labia. I instinctually lean in and move my body in a rhythmic motion with his large finger.

After a minute, he pulls his finger away and puts it in his mouth while he looks at me.

I love this strange obsession he has with bodily fluids.

His eyes are dark with his desire, and my heart is pounding. I can't believe this is finally happening. I'm so excited I'm trembling.

Those grey alien eyes go to my breasts, and his fingers follow. He pinches both of my nipples forcefully and moves my breasts up and down, "So human."

I can feel the moisture between my legs on the top of my thighs and the throbbing of my sex. I want this so much.

Suddenly, his mouth is on one of my breasts, and his other finger has found my clit, he's lightly tracing it with his finger as he pulls at my nipple with his mouth.

I can't help it. I put my hand on the back of his head. My fingers are intertwined in his long braid. I have never touched him like this before and I know from watching him with the prostitutes he doesn't like this.

Seb takes his hand from my clit.

I don't move, for fear I have ruined this. After a few seconds, I breathe out as I realize he is only undoing his braid. He lets his beautiful long black hair loose as is his custom when he goes to sleep, and then his hand goes back to my clit, and his mouth moves up my neck.

"Breath, Ensley," he says softly in my ear.

I jerk almost coming from the excitement of it all. His breath on my ear is so sensual.

Seb gently pushes me back on his bed and puts his head between my thighs. He separates my folds with his long tongue and begins licking. Long licks, short licks, sucking, and a little nibbling.

I'm in ecstasy. I don't know if I should tell him if I'm going to come or not. But then I think *I'm a pet, he doesn't expect me to, does he?* In the heat of the moment, I can't help myself, "Please don't stop." I don't even know if I am speaking his language or my own his tongue feels so good. I almost wonder if it's all a dream.

Thankfully it isn't a dream, and Seb doesn't stop, and within seconds, he has me writhing with pleasure. Even after I come, he still doesn't stop with his tongue, and pleasure turns to agony.

I want him to move away, but he won't. I'm becoming sore until the pain begins to become a pleasure again, and he's bringing me to orgasm again. My clit is raw and tingly with the ecstasy of it, my whole labia is on fire with desire and I come harder than I had the first time, which I didn't even think was possible. I see stars like I have a migraine, but this is anything but pain.

After he brings me to come a second time, Seb moves away from me on the bed, "Ensley, stay." He stands up and strips off his uniform.

I've seen my master naked every day, but now watching him reveal his naked flesh, it feels like the first time I see him. This is his choice to have sex with me, and I'm beyond thrilled. I would wag my tail aggressively if I were a dog, so I do the next best thing a human pet can do, I clench my vagina on the naked, cold air in anticipation when I see his massive penis when he removes his trousers.

Seb moves to the side of the bed, flips me over, holds my wrists behind me, and without a word, inserts his large penis into my wet vagina and begins to pound into me like a dog at the park, and I love it. I love the way he is holding my hands behind my back tightly and just takes me.

I'm coming again. His penis filling me and touching every inch of me feels like heaven. "Faster," I pant, but he doesn't respond, and I shut my mouth for fear he will stop if I speak again. I know that right now it has to be his way. He is my master, and I am his pet. And I'm a very happy pet. *Yes, yes, yes,* I keep thinking with every thrust. *I never care if I see Earth again.* This final act of him taking me like this makes my body orgasm again. I can think of nothing but him inside of me, nailing my core, making me fully submit.

When Seb finishes, he lies down for just a second next to me on his bed, to catch his breath, then he picks me up and puts me into my bed without saying anything, only patting me on the head.

Afterward, he crawls into his bed and goes to sleep.

I watch him and then close my eyes, wondering what just took place and what his plans for me are. Obviously to have a child but for what? More pets to give out to the crew? But that doesn't make sense because they would be his children too. I absently watch Seb's sleeping form while I try to figure out his intentions.

THE NEXT MORNING, Seb wakes me up by picking me up and taking me into the shower. He takes my body under the cold water with him and, again, without much preparation, takes my wrists, turns me around, and plunges his penis in and out of me as the cool water pours down on us. My face and breasts are pushed up against the cold stone wall while he plunges deep. It feels so good.

He keeps saying, "My little pet."

And I love it because it's so wrong. I control myself not to bark.

After Seb comes, he washes me and then himself with soap. When we are clean and dry, he picks me up and puts me back in bed and pats my head.

I watch him put on his uniform as he leaves to go on duty, and then I close my eyes, content.

The young man wakes me at his usual time and takes me to the toilet to pee and then gets me dressed. I wonder how much Seb tells him because even though my hair is dry, he obviously knows I've had a shower. I try to ask the young man about this, but he just shakes his head at me, clearly not wanting to talk about it.

I'm disappointed by this as the young man is usually so talkative to me. He more than anyone else has taught me the most Imperial and is the most patient with me when I have questions about the language or culture or if I need help with pronunciation.

He puts my leash on and takes me for my usual walk. I don't know why, but I don't want any of the other men touching me, only Seb. However, when I resist, I'm punished for it by the men slapping my sensitive vulva, reminding me to be a good human. They don't strike me hard, though, and I know they must be disappointed, but for two days, Seb has given me what I needed, so I'm no longer parading around the ship like a dog in heat.

After my afternoon nap, Seb comes back to his quarters, and without saying anything to me takes me from behind again. He doesn't even bother to remove his uniform. I'm already wet from all the men touching me on my walk around the ship, despite my protests. *The body will do what the body will do*, I think.

Seb finally says, "I heard you resisted my men petting you today. If it happens again, I'll punish you."

"Yes, Seb," I breathe out between taking his hard thrusts into me.

"You are my little human pet, and it makes everyone happy to rub your fur and give you attention. It's good for morale."

"Yes, Seb."

"Good," he says, holding me so tight as he uses me more roughly than ever before.

I'm sure my wrists will have bruises on them later.

When he's finished, he brings me to my knees, "Clean me, Ensley."

I look at his still throbbing penis and then bring it to my mouth with my hand.

"Just use your mouth."

I do as he bids, although it is a little tricky as his penis is still jerking, and it hits my cheek before I can manage to take it in my mouth.

Seb takes a sharp intake of breath, "Good, hot-mouthed human. Gods, yes, get my penis clean with your tongue."

When I'm finished, Seb is hard again. He picks me up without any effort and takes me to his bed. He lies down and puts me on top of him. Facing him. "Ensley, go up and down so I can see your breasts bounce."

Again, I do as I am bid. It feels so good. His erect penis inside of me. My clit rubbing against his skin. His hands firmly on my breasts, squeezing, and pulling.

"Ride me faster, pet."

I do my best to do as he asks, but I want to go slow. I want to ride out my next orgasm looking at him, my alien master.

Seb lets go of my breasts and moves his hands to my hips, grabbing them firmly, and then moves me up and down, "Good. That's it. I love the way your human breasts move."

I let him do this until he has come again, "Now," he said, bringing out a little device I've never seen before, "stay still."

I am, of course, very nervous about any devices he has as I assume; they are all punishment devices, so I shake my head.

"No, Ensley," he says in his usual tone, and I try not to back away.

I'm scared, so I move away from him on the large bed, still shaking my head.

"Do you want to be punished?"

"I do not," I reply. Still looking at the device warily.

"Come here," he commands.

I hang my head and move back towards him on the bed. He could have easily grabbed me himself, but of course, this is a power game.

When I get back to my original position, I watch him attach the device close to the outer rim of my vagina. It looks like a little robotic bug.

He grabs my arms with one hand to keep me on the bed as I can't help myself and scream at the sight of the little robotic bug.

"Stay Ensley. This won't hurt, quite the opposite."

I pause then, hoping he isn't lying to me. Then I can feel the robot bug moving, and I close my eyes, hoping this isn't some sick fetish with bugs. I keep telling myself, *At least it's not a real bug, just a little robot.*

Seb is petting my hair with his other hand, "Good Ensley. Let the little bug bring you the greatest satisfaction."

The robot bug makes me orgasm again and again and again. It doesn't stop. I have no control over it, and I'm paralyzed from the extreme pleasure. All the while Seb is looking into my eyes watching me and stroking my hair. I can't even begin to wonder what the point of this would be.

When I finally stop orgasming, I still can't move, and I'm so shaky I just lie there on his bed. Seb picks me up and puts me in my little bed, where I promptly fall asleep.

THE NEXT DAYS and weeks are roughly all the same.

This morning, when the young man takes me for my regular morning walk around the ship, we stop by sickbay. It doesn't occur to me that I could be pregnant as I have not had a period since I had been taken by the other green aliens or 'the puppy pound' as I call them. I had assumed that when they had done that first medical check on me, if we want to call it that, they had taken my uterus. I didn't want to mention this to Seb because I figured he already knew or if he didn't know he wouldn't want to have sex with me if I told him.

The young man leads me into sickbay and makes me lie down on a medical bed. We must wait for the doctor to finish with another patient before he condescends to come over to us. We silently watch the doctor and I look at the young man, I think he must feel the same as me, annoyed the doctor is taking his sweet time in coming over.

When he finally does come over, he doesn't greet the young man or me, he just begins running scans, and then he says out-of-the-blue, "Good human. You are bred." Then he pets my vulva way more than he should and walks away.

The young man puts his hand on my back, encouraging me to sit up, attaches my leash, and we continue our walk around the ship in silence.

That evening when Seb comes back to his quarters, he tells me he has a surprise for me.

He dresses me in the outfit that shows off not only my fur as he likes to call it but also my breasts and then takes me to an area of the ship I have never been to before. It looks like the inside of a castle, everything is stone, and there are no windows. I don't know what this room is or what it might be used for. Inside are lots of his officers. He leads me in by my leash, and lots of his men approach us, all petting my vulva and playing with my breasts. Again, I'm becoming so sexually frustrated. I'm used to getting sex now, but all I want is for Seb to take me back to his quarters and relieve this need. I don't want any of these men touching me and I don't want to have a gangbang.

I look at Seb, and he seems pleased. I don't understand why he thinks I would want this. I try to give him a look that says, I'm-unhappy-with-this.

He gives me a confused look in reply.

My heart sinks. I return his confused look, thinking, *How can you be confused? I want only you.* Then I remind myself, *He bought me for himself and the men. He's told me that.* I try not to cry over this. I try to focus on my role now, which includes letting his officers touch me, but it's difficult. I don't want this, I only want Seb.

After about an hour of alien men fondling me, Seb takes me to another area of the ship that I'm familiar with, the religious shrine. While there, Seb lights a candle and says some prayers in front of a statue while I wait at his feet. There is a priest who is occasionally here.

I don't like the priest because he has greedy hands and unfortunately, he is here today. While Seb is praying, the priest makes me stand, and he fondles my breasts and then puts his hand between my legs, "Captain, she is so wet. Is she always like this?"

"Almost always," Seb replies casually.

I want to shout, 'And I'm all his so get your greedy hands off me,' but I know I can't. So, I let the priest touch me, and I sadly remind myself, *I'm only a pet to Seb.*

Then the priest begins rubbing my clit in circular motions, "That's it. Good human."

I don't want his hands on me, but after a few minutes, I do want to orgasm. I look over at Seb, and he seems turned on by the priest getting me off, so I let it happen. I think about Seb's feelings rather than my own. I come right there all over the priest's hand.

Afterward, he says to Seb, "She smells so sweet. Maybe when I get enough UCs, I'll get a human too. Your quarters must smell like paradise, Captain."

I am, of course, humiliated now that my need has been fulfilled by the covetous priest, but I don't have much time to think about it because soon Seb is taking me somewhere else. After walking for five minutes, we arrive at a small dark room with a stone floor. I know enough about their culture now to know this must be a sacred room, like the religious shrine, because I smell the same incense, but there are no religious statues here and no furniture.

After a few minutes of being alone with Seb, some of his good friends, including the doctor, come in.

Seb turns to me, not letting go of my leash, "This is your surprise. We are all going to quench this human vagina." His fingers slip in and then circles my vagina as he speaks the last sentence.

I'm dumbfounded. I look at the men and then back at Seb, terrified. I've never had a threesome, let alone a sexual encounter with four men. And these aren't just men, they are four big grey aliens. I quickly run behind Seb to hide.

Seb laughs and brings me back around with gentle force, "Don't worry, Ensley, no one will hurt you. You are always so shy, but I know you'll love this. Humans love sex."

The men all move in, circling me. They have all stripped off their clothing, large penises erect and ready, closing in on me. My heart is beating so loudly, I can hardly hear Seb say, "The priest couldn't help himself and already made her come once."

The doctor hastily takes my leash as Seb undresses.

Two men are playing with my breasts as another puts his mouth on my clit, and my fear is vanishing. It's being replaced by pleasure, and I wonder how I could have been afraid of this before? I look at Seb and tell myself, *He would never let anything bad happen to me.* Why he would think I would want a gangbang, I don't know. Imperial culture is strange and has even stranger customs surrounding sex. *Thankfully, there are no other humans here,* I think.

Then my thoughts return to Hillbilly, like a scratch on my favorite record, and I wonder if she is being used by the Octopods like this. I shudder to think about multiple tentacles with suckers all touching every part of my body, even up my vagina and in my mouth choking me. I quickly banish that image from my mind, and then I'm grateful that at least these aliens look like men and are respectful. I have never feared for my life here. With that thought, I try to enjoy myself. I can't close my eyes as that's rude, but I keep my sight firmly locked on Seb. He is my everything, and at least now he is participating. I root my thoughts there. I imagine every one of these men is an extension of my master. His eight arms, forty fingers, four tongues, and four penises.

I freeze when a finger is inserted in my anus. I want to say, 'That's a one-way hole,' but I know they would only laugh, and I'd probably be punished for talking, so I don't say anything, but I keep trying to move the fingers away with my hands. Unfortunately, the men sucking and kneading my breasts causally takes my wrists and holds them loosely so I can't move. Gradually, there are fingers in my anus and vagina and what feels like mouths everywhere. I remind myself that all of these appendages belong to Seb, eight arms, forty fingers, four tongues, and four penises.

I tense as the finger on my rear pushes further in. I've always heard anal sex hurt. I have heard horror stories about porn stars needing reconstructive surgery after anal sex gangbangs. If I didn't allow my human boyfriend with his small penis in there, I'm certainly not allowing giant aliens organs in there. But just as I start to really protest the finger in my anus, Seb is there, his breath on my ear as he speaks. I've goosebumps from him talking to me so closely, "Ensley, you need to relax. Relax. This is your next task on your path to be the perfect pet. You want that, don't you?"

Of course, I want that. I want to please Seb more than anything, "It'll hurt." I don't know how to say, 'I'm afraid.' I don't have the vocabulary as the word, 'afraid 'doesn't come up in Imperial conversation. These aliens aren't afraid of anything, it seems.

As the fingers begin to move in and out of my anus. I try to relax and remind myself repeatedly, *Seb wants this. It will make him so happy. Lots of women do it.*

My mind is on a track of its own now, and I don't know why but I think of Hillbilly again and how she screamed as she was dragged out, *And I never heard of anal sex killing anyone.*

The men are working me. I keep reminding myself that it's all for Seb.

They keep calling me their 'adorable human' and telling me I'm a 'good human pet.' It's everything I want to hear. I come so hard with these men's hands and mouths on me I would have collapsed if they had not been holding me up. When I come back around to only a half lusty haze, I'm led to an area of the stone floor and pushed back on top of Seb. "I'm going to put myself in your anus."

Knowing how big his penis is, I really don't want it there. I shake my head.

"No, Ensley," he says.

I can tell by the look on his face that I'm embarrassing him by not just doing what he wants, but fingers up my butt were one thing, his enormous penis followed by these men's penises is another. My fears of needing reconstructive surgery after an anal alien gangbang return.

Seb gets up, places my hands on the stone wall, and bends me over. He then begins spanking me. Each slap sends pain coursing through my body, and the sound echoes in the stone room. My rear is on fire.

"I know you can do better." He slaps me again, "Are you going to obey? Are you going to be my perfect human pet?"

"Yes, Seb," I say. I want to be that for him.

Seb takes my shaky hand and lies back down on the stone floor and guides me on top of him. He begins inserting his penis into my anus.

It hurts. Even though he had covered his penis in something slick, it still hurts a lot, and I have to hold my breath not to cry out. I bite my lip, and I'm sure I'm drawing blood. Then another man lies on top of me and begins using my vagina slowly.

All so slowly, but all I want is for all of this to end. I can feel their penises threaten to rip my thin skin between my vagina and anus apart. I try not to cry. But then at some point, this all shifts from pain to pleasure, and I begin to derive pleasure from Seb and the other men using both my holes. It is so strange, and I just let myself go, and I'm gone. I have no more thoughts, just sensual bodies, pleasure, and pain. I half wonder at one point if I've died.

I've closed my eyes and imagined Seb's eight arms, forty fingers, four tongues, and four penises throughout this slow double-penetration that is both strange and somewhat enjoyable.

Seb is the only one who put his penis in my anus and the only man who comes inside of my vagina. The others just watch their penises still erect. I thought they would have the opportunity to be with me as well, but I am, of course, happy they don't, even if I don't understand why not. *This is such a strange alien culture*, I think, as Seb leads me out of the sacred room by my leash after it's ended.

Semen and my own wetness are running down my thighs from my vagina and anus. I feel gross. All I want now is a shower.

Thankfully, there aren't many people in the hallway, but the ones we pass stop to touch me. I try to back away, but Seb doesn't let me and has a harsh word when I try.

It's so strange, these men feel nothing about touching another man's semen on me, especially with the peculiar way they feel about bodily fluids. They only smile and laugh.

I wonder then, *How much of this culture am I missing?* I realize that I'm so clouded by my human understanding of things that I can't hope to understand what's happening here. I thought I had some understanding after all the months I've been immersed here, but what's happening now doesn't make any sense. I feel confused.

When we arrive back in Seb's quarters, he picks me up gently, but unnecessarily and carries me into the shower. As we stand in the freezing shower, he tells me I'm a good human, repeatedly. This isn't his usual behavior, and I wonder if he feels guilty for sharing me like a whore, knowing I didn't want to be shared.

I don't feel like a good pet and I begin to cry, and once I start, I can't' stop. I cry for everything that has happened, everything that's happening now and all the other bad stuff that I'm sure will happen in the future. I want to go home. I know I can't say that to Seb, but I'm crying so hard, I probably couldn't say the words even if I had the courage to because I'm having such an ugly cry.

Seb holds me against his naked body under the cold water.

I shake with my tears and the cold water.

He holds me close for so long, I imagine I'm not his pet, but his lover or his wife. It is that kind of embrace and I compose myself.

When I'm led out into the bedroom, the doctor stands up. I freeze. I don't want to see him or any of the other men. I want to forget this night ever happened.

"It's okay, Ensley," Seb says, patting me on the head. Then he goes to where he keeps a little bit of my chocolate and brings me some.

I take it and automatically eat it while he and the doctor talk.

"She's very sad now," Seb says as if he is surprised that I'd be unhappy he basically introduced me to an anal gangbang with his friends.

"This isn't uncommon with human pets. It's because she has a little one growing inside of her. Don't worry, we can make her better."

"Please," Seb gestures to me.

I eye the doctor while still eating my chocolate. He comes over with a little medical polymer in his hand. Of course, I want to back away from him, but I know that'll only make Seb annoyed.

"Ensley, I'm just going to check your anus and vagina to make sure everything is fine. After our fun," the doctor almost laughs, and I 'accidentally' kick him. I didn't do it hard enough for him to care.

"Calm yourself. Ensley, I'm here to help." He speaks the words kindly now.

The doctor's sympathetic voice after I kick him brings on a whole new wave of tears as a reminder of how confusing all of this is. I can't help myself, I start to cry again.

I look at Seb, and he gives me a worried look.

I think, *Really? You don't understand that I don't like other men's hands on me? You alien pervert.*

The doctor is gently and methodically checking my body for injury. I feel him do something, and then I have no pain, except, of course, the pain and shame in my heart.

The doctor then looks into my eyes and pats my head, "It's okay. Maybe in time, you will understand. You are a good human, Ensley."

I want to ask what I'll understand in time and how he knows what I'm thinking, but I don't bother because I know my language wouldn't be good enough to understand this cultural norm that I am obviously missing.

"What about a knowledge download?" Seb asks.

"No," the doctor says, rubbing my vulva lightly like he is petting a dog, "I'm afraid it would be too much for her human brain. It would only make things worse; she might even go mad from it."

The doctor backs away from me then and talks to Seb. I don't listen because I don't care. They aren't talking about me anymore anyway. I just want to sleep. I look over longingly at my bed. I want to just go there, but I know if I do, Seb will reprimand me because he likes to say when I should go to bed.

I wait in the center of the room. After about fifteen minutes have passed, I lie down on the floor while they are still talking.

I must have fallen asleep because when I wake up, Seb is carrying me to my little bed.

He tucks me in as usual, and I fall into a dreamless sleep, wanting to escape the memories of today.

CHAPTER 6

eb

I LIE on the side of my bed and watch Ensley sleep. I worry that I've done something wrong. I thought the look she gave me in the intimacy room was one of shyness. I assumed that once the sex began that she would enjoy herself. However, I was wrong.

I have followed all the instructions from the human-pet experts, but something nags at the edge of my thoughts. I remember one of the experts explicitly saying that even the best trainers are incapable of teaching some humans as a few simply lack the intelligence to learn.

I don't think Ensley is unintelligent. She has learned the Imperial language faster than the experts said she would. She has shown me on a few occasions that she has a memory longer than two days and she seems to understand her position on the ship. However, tonight was a disaster. I thought she would have been pleased to have so much sex. The human-pet experts all agree that humans love sex with multiple partners, and do not have the capacity to feel things such as shame or embarrassment when it comes to bodily pleasure. However, after what I witnessed tonight, I would strongly disagree. Ensley clearly showed a preference for me and was traumatized that I introduced her to sex with my friends. I'm sure the human-pet experts would tell me that this is because I've been too gentle with her, that I've changed her nature. But in turn, I would ask them if it's possible that this has always been her nature and that we, Imperial people, may be mistreating pets. That it could be possible that humans have evolved into more sentient beings?

I question myself, *What makes a conscious and sentient being? Being able to talk and verbalize thoughts, Ensley does that to a certain degree. I wish that she had a translator, then I would know if she has more complex thoughts, if she really has full self-awareness or if this is all instinct. I want to know if she forgets details of her life every second day. I want to know if she was shamed or just afraid in the intimacy room.*

The doctor has assured me that there is no need to worry. He says her crying is a reaction to her body's hormonal changes. He recommended medicine Imperial women take for this same condition, and I have agreed that Ensley should take it. I sincerely hope that after a good rest and continued use of the medicine, she will feel better. *Less fearful and less shy*, I think.

I can't sleep. So, I sit at my desk in the other room searching for information about humans who cry a lot. I don't learn anything new. According to the experts, I haven't done anything terribly wrong in Ensley's training except possibly being too gentle. As I listen to more, I am thankful that Ensley has never displayed the kind of naughty behavior some of the human experts talk about in their informational lessons as reasons to put your human down. After a few hours, I have no choice but to believe my doctor is correct and that her emotional outburst is only the hormones. However, I can't shake this nagging feeling that Ensley is a just as much a sentient being as I am, but I don't want to acknowledge this because I don't know if I would be able to live with myself, knowing that I bought a pet that is not a pet. Also knowing, I must keep a pet who is not a pet in captivity until the day she dies. The thought makes me nauseous, not only would I have wronged Ensley, but if it was true, I couldn't tell anyone about my discovery. If I did, they would say I had gone mad. Or blame my lack of wife for my anthropomorphizing Ensley.

Just before I am ready to try and sleep again, I happen across a lesson about human pregnancies and decide since it is short, I will watch it. It starts by stating that humans cannot give birth alone and need help, or they may die. Then it offers some useful information about how to know when your human is in labor and what to do. By the end, it says, during gestation, some humans become very emotional, and it is suggested that during this time, pets sleep with their masters for extra reassurance. The trainer finishes the lesson by reminding pet owners that even though co-sleeping seems ridiculous to us, it provides a great comfort to humans who are still closer to their primate ancestors than evolved Imperial people.

Resolute now, I turn off my computer and go back into the bedroom. I get into my bed and my eyes wonder over to Ensley curled up in her little bed. All I can see of her are some yellow strands of hair peeking out as she prefers to sleep with the blankets completely covering her head.

After a few seconds of contemplation, I go to her, pick her up gently, and bring her into my bed. It feels better than I thought it would to have her next to me. I fall asleep with my hand on her small warm hip.

IN THE MORNING, when I wake, the smell of Ensley is all around me. Instinctively, my hands find her human breasts. I hold one in each hand, kneading them and pulling on her nipples. I do this for a while until I am sure she is awake. Then I lie on my back and place her on top of me and can't help but think, *Maybe having her next to me when I wake up isn't such an inconvenience.*

However, when we make eye contact, I remember her face from last night and I ask, "Ensley, you can say 'no.'"

She looks at me blankly and I wonder if she even remembers what happened yesterday.

I don't move.

Ensley is sitting on me.

We are staring at each other.

I'm inside of her and it takes all of my control not to move in some way. I'm trying to figure out what she wants.

Ensley takes my hands and puts them on her hips and begins to move on top of me.

I urge her to go faster and faster until I get what I want.

Then, I lift her off me, and put my head between her thighs. I lick every part of her, only using my hands to still her body so I can be sure she gets what she wants as well. When I am satisfied that she is sated, I tuck her up in my bed, just the way she likes it with the blankets covering every inch of her and go get ready for my day.

As I leave my quarters, I send a message to my squire, letting him know that I have brought Ensley into my bed and not to punish her for breaking the rules.

Then I go to the bridge. I don't want to be here. I think way too much about Ensley because we are in no man's land, and there is nothing to do or see. The only other starships we've passed have been on long range sensors. Our mission was to investigate a decimated science station on the edge of Imperial space only to find out they had probably been hit by a stray asteroid by just being in the wrong place at the wrong time. There were no signs of foul play in the debris. It goes without saying that this has been a long and tedious mission that is not over. It will still be months until we return to the inner circle of galactic civilization.

After a mind-numbingly dull day, I am happy to return to Ensley, who thankfully seems much happier today.

"Hi Seb," she greets me as she usually does, and I touch her silky yellow hair.

"Ensley, I'll give you some chocolate if you can listen to my words." I want to try to talk to her about yesterday. I want to know if she even remembers yesterday or if I really am losing my mind.

Ensley nods.

I lead her by taking her wrist loosely into the sitting area. I indicate she should sit on the floor and I sit in the chair, as we usually do. "Tell me about yesterday."

"Yesterday?" she seems confused.

I don't know if she knows this word, so I painfully say, "Before the long sleep. Yesterday."

"Yesterday," she says the word slowly and then asks, "What?"

"You were crying."

She looks down at the floor but doesn't speak.

After a minute, I ask her, "Do you remember crying? Look at me."

Ensley looks up at me, almost guilty, but I think I must be imagining it. "I'm sorry. I ..."

"It's okay if you can't remember," I reassure her.

"No, I..." she begins again and then is concentrating searching for a word perhaps, "I want to be good, but I only want you. I don't understand."

"You remember yesterday?"

"Yes, Seb."

"You only want me to touch you that's why you were crying?"

"Yes." She looks down at the floor again.

I pet her hair. Then I get up and retrieve a bit of chocolate from the dining room and give to her, she seems genuinely confused, but takes it.

I watch her eat the chocolate and then ask, "You don't want to have sex with a lot of men?"

She stops eating and looks up at me terrified.

"It's okay. You can tell me."

She doesn't seem convinced or she doesn't understand.

I begin to wonder if she knows what we are talking about. I sigh and touch her head, "It's okay, you're a good human." I don't want to stress her out by talking about things she can't understand.

AFTER DINNER AND HER WALK, I want to go to the doctor's for a few drinks, but she pulls hard on her leash when she realized where we were headed. I'm so surprised she remembers I want to ask her if she really knew where we were headed, but before I can she takes my hand and puts it to her wet sex.

I can't resist her.

We walk back to my quarters and on the way, I tell the doctor that I'm not coming.

He laughs and tells me spending too much time alone with Ensley will lead to madness. This comment hits me hard as I'm beginning to think he is right.

When we return, I strip off her clothing and then mine.

I bend her over the bed, then I lick her anus and vagina. She seems to stiffen, but I won't be deterred.

I put my finger in her anus while rubbing her clitoris. She moans, and then I bring her to climax. It wasn't difficult. *Humans are so sexual,* I think and wonder again if it was just her shyness that made her uncomfortable with the other men.

I thrust my penis into her warm and wet vagina, wondering how I would ever find an Imperial woman's vagina pleasurable again after the heat of my human. Before I am going to come, I rescind and then enter her anus. I hear her gasp and put my hand on her clitoris to ease her. Then I thrust in and out of her anus until I come.

I don't know why I wanted to come in her anus. But I know I am lying to myself. I know I wanted to do it to maintain dominance over her. I love Ensley to be sure, but she is my pet. I'm concerned with how often my thoughts are centered around her and how I'm beginning to question the human-pet experts. I'm anthropomorphizing Ensley, and I need to stop.

OVER THE NEXT MONTHS, Ensley shares my bed every night. I have sex with her often, and she likes it. My friends ask if they can have sex with her again, and I tell them to wait. I don't want to make her sad again. I still have not been able to figure out why she didn't like having sex with so many men.

Ensley's abdomen is growing with our hybrid baby, and her clothing doesn't fit anymore, so she is often naked except for her leash. On her walks around the ship, everyone admires her beautiful body. I am always proud of her, and she behaves so well these days. I can't decide if it's because of the daily sex, that she's excited to be pregnant or if it's because she is sleeping in my bed.

Tonight, before we fall asleep, she is looking at me funny, "What Ensley?"

She touches her extended abdomen, "What will happen to this baby? Will it be a pet like me?"

"No, it will be Imperial."

"Can I keep it?"

I was surprised by her question. The human experts had said humans didn't care for their offspring, so it wasn't a problem to take it away from them after the weaning period. "For a little while," I answer her and watch Ensley's reaction. She seems content with my answer, so I assume she only meant the weaning period.

I LOOK over at Ensley on the sofa. I allow her to relax there now while I work because it's uncomfortable for her on the floor where she would normally sit now that she is so pregnant. I notice that she has become big not only where the baby is growing but everywhere else as well. I've stopped giving her chocolates and human food to make sure she doesn't eat too much but she still seems to be getting bigger.

I've asked my doctor about it and he says it's absolutely fine and that it is probably a good idea to stop giving her human food now as it's not as healthy as Imperial food.

I've also instructed my squire not to give her extra food at mealtimes. However, she is still growing everywhere.

She looks up at me because she could feel my eyes on her, "What Seb?"

"I'm worried about your eating," I admit.

"Is it mealtime?"

I realize she has not understood me, but I don't try to explain. The concept of becoming overweight and that being unhealthy may be completely unknown to humans. I just smile, "Not yet."

. . .

I FINISH the meeting early and then hurry to sickbay. Ensley should still be having her check up with the doctor. I walk in and see Ensley sitting on the edge of the medical bed naked and the doctor putting chocolates into her mouth, while my squire watches with a smile on his face.

It takes all my self-control not to yell at the doctor, but I can't help but say sternly, "I thought you said it was good that we stop feeding her human food."

The doctor, clearly startled by my entrance, smiles, "I said it was good for *you* to stop feeding her human food. It's okay if the rest of us do it," he says and gives Ensley another piece of chocolate directly into her open mouth.

"What do you mean, 'the rest of us'? Who else is giving her food?"

"Oh, I don't know names," replies the doctor.

I look at my squire and he looks at his feet, "Well, I would appreciate if you and these other nameless people would stop feeding her. She's my pet and I don't want her getting fat."

Ensley gives me an adorably pitiful look.

The doctor pats her head, "Oh Captain, she's not going to get fat. You know she's eating for two and it makes her so happy when we give her the chocolate. Just look at her."

I look at Ensley and then back to the doctor, "You of all people know better than to overfeed her."

I take Ensley's leash and attach it around her neck and then lead her back to my quarters with my squire. Later that night I make it clear that if I catch anyone feeding Ensley besides myself or my squire, punishments will follow.

Ensley looks guilty as I announce this to my crew. I tell her afterward, "It's not your fault. You don't know what's good for you."

I BELIEVE that it's the lack of sex that makes her want to eat so much. So I organize some of my friends to play with her. I have told them all in advance that she doesn't like anal sex. Even though she has not cried when I do it, I will never forget the look on her face last time.

When I told her about tonight, I was baffled that she wasn't more excited. As I understand it, humans love sex and would do it with anyone if not trained. Ensley is always aroused, even from the slightest attention from the men, so I thought she would enjoy this, "Do you want more men?"

She shakes her head.

"I don't understand, Ensley. I know you like sex. This should be fun for you."

She touches her abdomen, "I worry about the baby."

"It will be fine. The doctor will be there and we will all be very careful. Come now. The men have been fantasizing about this for weeks now. There's nothing quite like a human."

Ensley is naked except for her leash, and I lead her into the intimacy room. My friends are already there. Someone has brought an Imperial woman who has warm oil with her.

The Imperial woman comes to Ensley and takes her leash then rubs oil all over Ensley's skin while the men take off their clothes and watch.

Ensley looks like she enjoys the Imperial woman's touch, and I am happy to see it.

I physically see Ensley begin to relax.

When the Imperial woman is finished with Ensley, she calls me forward and starts putting oil all over my body then tells me I am ready. I rub my body next to Ensley, both of us slippery with the oil, and then I find her wet entrance and thrust into her.

I grab her hips and pound as hard as I can into her. It feels so good not only because it is Ensley, and I can always do this, but because I can also share her with my friends.

Then they each have a turn, taking care to be especially gentle with Ensley. They make her come again and again. I feel like everyone is having a good time as it should be. The Imperial woman even wants a turn, and I allow it, even though on planet it's I who must share myself with women and in space women who must share themselves with men. We are all aroused again by watching the two women, writhing against one another.

In the end, there is both female and male fluids everywhere, and everyone seems satisfied. I put on my clothes and lead Ensley back to my quarters. I take a shower with her, hoping that she will not cry like last time, and she doesn't which is a relief. She seems fine, and I wonder if the anal sex was so painful for her and that her true nature is to really love sex like all the human-pet experts say.

After our shower, I put her into my bed, and go to do some work in the sitting room.

By the time I lay down to sleep, Ensley is asleep but restless. She is tossing and turning and crying out in her human language.

I try to comfort her. I stroke her hair and say, "It's okay, you are safe with me," but when I touch her, she wakes up.

She opens her eyes and looks at me with pain, "I hurt."

I sit up and ask where.

She cradles her abdomen. For fear of the baby, I call the doctor to my quarters immediately.

* * *

Ensley

I WAKE up to Seb trying to comfort me. I want to tell him that I think the baby is coming, but on the other hand, I don't mind letting the doctor do some extra leg work. I almost smile thinking about the doctor having to get up out of bed in the middle of the night come here and then go to sickbay.

The best part about being a pet is not having to do much, I think, as I'm carried to sickbay. I look up at Seb's face as he carries me, and he's very concerned. I like this. Ever since he has allowed me to sleep in his bed, my life has been almost perfect. When we lie together uncon-scious, and his hand rests on my hip, I can imagine, during the sleeping hours, that I'm his wife, not his pet, and that we have a real relationship. That he really cares for me as an equal. I enjoy reveling in this fantasy every night, and as it's still the middle of the night, I consider this time still my fantasy time. Then another contraction hits me, and I close my eyes and lose that train of thought.

Finally, we reach sickbay, and Seb lays me down on a medical bed. I look at all the medical equipment and hope Imperial people have something to take the edge off these contractions. They're an advanced species with spaceships and all kinds of crazy technology, surely, they have managed to make childbirth less painful or not painful at all.

I look up at Seb in between contractions, "Medicine?" I try to pronounce the word correctly, but I know this particular word has a sound in it I can't really make. Seb has to ask me three times what I want, and I start to question whether or not he's the stupid one.

"No," he says when he finally understands. "Bad for the baby," he tells me gently.

I reply in English, "You've got to be kidding me!" All the men in sickbay just look at me, and then, I say in their language, quietly, hoping to gain more sympathy, "I hurt Seb."

The doctor and Seb start talking heatedly, I can't understand everything they are saying but I know against the doctor's better judgment, I'm given some medicine. The dose is so effective that suddenly I feel no pain at all. It disappeared.

But I'm not in a drug haze or anything that I would have expected from a human medicine. I'm vigilant and aware, just separated from the pain. I feel like a superhero. It's crazy because I know my body is hurting.

I feel the contractions, but they only feel like vibrations. My body has become a machine that I'm monitoring.

I had expected the doctor to help me to know when to push, as that's what I had seen in all the movies, but when I get the urge to push, I ask him for guidance.

"Only you and your body know. You can feel it, right?"

I can tell by the look on his face and the look that he gives to Seb that he's very concerned that giving me the medicine, which I'm sure is only for Imperial women, is going to hinder me delivering this baby. I want to tell him that, of course, I feel like pushing but that on Earth, we rely on doctors to tell us when it's okay to do so, or so I thought. What do I know about having a baby? He's the doctor.

The doctor is worried about me. He brings out some more medical equipment while mumbling to himself.

I realize then that doctor isn't so bad, just probably socially awkward, even among his own people. I look up at Seb, and he's worried too.

I smile at Seb and say, "I know when to push." I don't explain how I thought it should be.

Seb nods at me but doesn't smile back.

The doctor comes to my side, "Do you feel like pushing Ensley?"

I nod.

"Then do it and find a position that feels good." When he notices that I don't understand, he clarifies, "You can go anywhere. Stand anyway."

I'd lying on the medical bed, but when he mentions that I should find a good position, I decide I want to walk around. I've always thought women lay on their backs to have babies, because of television, but that's the last thing I feel like to doing right now. I don't feel any pain, but I can feel the baby coming with the vibration of the contracts, and I feel like pushing with them. It's so very odd.

I walk around sickbay and take in the strangeness of my situation. I'm naked and having a hybrid baby surrounded by grey aliens who are all looking at me as if I'm going to catch fire. "I'm okay," I say to Seb and the doctor.

Seb nods again.

The doctor continues to look at one of his small devices and says unnecessarily, "You are fine."

I want to slap him for mansplaining me, but I can't be sure that's what he's doing because my medical language is almost non-existent in Imperial, and he could be just confirming for Seb. I've a sneaking suspicion that in their culture, a woman would die rather than admit defeat.

As the contractions get closer, although I don't feel any pain, I feel the strongest urge to push and primal desire to see the baby. Throughout these last months, I've often wondered what it will look like. If it will have any human qualities to it or if Seb's Imperial genes will be entirely dominant.

I put my hands on the side of a medical bed to balance myself, squat and start to really push.

I don't care about the sounds I'm making, my body is telling me what to do, and I'm doing it. I'm like a goddam superhero.

The doctor is next to me. He's surprisingly not intrusive. Everyone else is quiet and respectful, and all focused on me.

I don't know why but a thought occurs to me, and I almost laugh, *Are they filming this for a human nature show?* But as soon as I think it, I forget it as I can feel that the baby is almost with me and all my concentration goes to my one and only task. I instinctively put my hand down and can feel the top of its little head. "It's head," I say in English. I think to myself, *This is the coolest thing I've ever done.*

I feel like I'm running a marathon, and sweat is pouring from me, but I still don't hurt.

I just feel pressure, and I know I need to push my baby out, which is the only thing I want in the entire galaxy right now. I smile at myself for thinking 'galaxy' rather than 'earth,' *I'm such a cosmopolitan pet*, I think.

It's not long before the little baby comes out. I sit back and take it in my arms. Its skin is grey and slimy. I don't know why, but I want to lick it. I don't do that, but instead, I hold it against my naked, sweaty body and bring it to my breast. The baby is wailing and peeing, and it's the most beautiful baby boy I've ever seen, "Look at you," I say. "You're so divine. Hush now, I've got you. The difficult part is over."

I count his tiny fingers and tiny toes, all grey like Seb's, but he's mine too somewhere in there. I'm relieved that he's a boy. I didn't want to know before because I didn't think I would have been able to push if it was a girl. I'd worry that she would be a pet like me, but worse, bred in captivity. I look down at my son and think, *He will never be used as I am.* I know the Empire rarely keeps males as pets.

Seb kneels next to me, "Good job, Ensley."

I can't help it. I smile up at him, my captor, my master, my lover, my fantasy husband. "Our baby," I say stupidly. I'm inarticulate in his language I can't say anything eloquent, not that Seb expects it, but I wish I could have said something more for myself. I've all these thoughts that he will never know about.

The doctor cuts the umbilical cord, and then I need to push again, the afterbirth. I reluctantly hand the baby to Seb and push.

When I look at the afterbirth, I think it looks like one of the more disgusting things I've ever seen in my life, and I move away from it. I try to stand, but I need assistance. Not because it hurts, I still don't feel anything, but because my legs won't hold me. With some help, I lie down on a medical bed, and then I say to Seb with outstretched hands, "Give me the baby."

I just lie there naked holding my baby, which someone has cleaned up. If I didn't know he was mine, I would think he was completely Imperial. Before I had him, I thought that if he came out like this, I wouldn't be able to love him, but now that he's here, and completely grey, I do love him. I can't help it. I love this little alien baby so much.

The doctor does some checks and runs some handheld devices over me and the baby, no doubt stitching me up or whatever they do in recovery. I only hope that when this pain medicine wears off that I won't be in too much pain. I look at the baby and think about the size of my vagina, *Yes, you probably stretched things until they ripped down there*. Half of me wanted to ask the doctor, but the other half told the first half to shut up because ignorance is bliss.

AFTER THE DOCTOR tells us we can go, Seb carries me and I'm holding the baby back to his quarters. I could have probably walked as I still don't feel anything, but I want Seb to carry me. When we enter his quarters, I notice that a little baby bed has appeared. Seb urges me to put the baby in the transparent bed.

"No, I want him next to me."

"No, Ensley," he taps the transparent bed. "This bed is connected to sickbay. If our baby becomes ill, the doctor will know."

Seb takes the baby from me and puts him in the transparent bed. Then looks back at me, "You understand? You cannot sleep with the baby. It is dangerous."

"Yes," I say, even though all my instincts are just the opposite. I can see Seb's logic, but in my heart, I just want to hold the baby.

I reluctantly get into Seb's bed, and he kindly pulls the transparent crib right next to me, so I can see the baby.

The baby is asleep, still all wound up like a ball like he's still inside of me. He doesn't have any clothing, but a little yellow fabric diaper that Seb has told me will clean itself.

I look at my little baby as I drift off to sleep. My hand on the top of the transparent crib so no one can take him from me while I sleep. In my mind, I call him 'Dylan.' I know Seb will probably give him an Imperial name, he may or may not tell me about, but just for me, this is what I'll call him.

I wake up to the baby crying just a few hours later. I know instinctively that he wants milk. I can hear it like I'm a baby whisperer or something. I'm naked, so it's no problem to pick up the baby and try to feed him. I look at the baby and my breast, and I hope this will work.

It seems like a simple thing in the movies, but just like everything, I suspect the movies lie, because they are written by men.

For a long time, the baby doesn't seem to understand what to do, Dylan just keeps crying and crying.

Now Seb is awake watching me. He doesn't seem surprised that breastfeeding isn't happening perfectly.

I wonder if he already has children. I'm very annoyed with the thought, "Do you know what to do?"

Seb shakes his head, "No, I've never been a father before. I thought breastfeeding happened naturally but be patient. The baby has your spirit, give him time. He will not starve yet as he has just left your body."

"My spirit?"

"Yes," Seb says as if he isn't being insulting at all, "persistent."

I look at him and ask, "What does 'persistent' mean?" I don't know this word in Imperial.

"You don't give up."

This is the greatest compliment I have ever received from anyone. I don't know why, but it feels so good to hear it. I turn my attention back to Dylan with new confidence. He's searching around my breast with his little head, I try to guide him, but in the end, I let him find my nipple with his jerky movements. When he doesn't realize he needs to suck. I gently rub his back, trying to be patient, wondering how long it'll take him to figure sucking out. I lean down and whisper, "Now you suck for the milk, little guy."

It seems like an eternity before Dylan figures out how to suck. And even then, I don't even know if any milk comes out, but he falls asleep at my breast.

I don't want to move him, but Seb, who has been patiently watching everything, insists I put him back in the alien crib.

"If you fall asleep, you could hurt him by mistake."

"It seems silly. He'll be hungry again soon," I protest.

"But it's safer," Seb says softly, taking Dylan from me.

THE DAYS melt into one another. Thankfully, my only task is taking care of Dylan, everyone else takes care of me. As little Dylan grows, I begin to see small traces of me in his appearance. His eyes are my green eyes, not only in color but in shape. I know from seeing some of the other Imperial men onboard that they could be the color of alien eyes too, but I tell myself his eyes are my eyes.

These similarities make me question whether humans have been interbred with Imperial people for so long that green eyes have come to them or to us through this interbreeding. Or if we are all the same kind of species, to begin with.

Looking at Dylan throughout the long hours of each day, I've had a lot of time to consider and question all the creation myths and science fiction I've ever heard about. I wonder if there's one master race that sprinkled DNA of humanity around the galaxy as a science experiment to see how we would all turn out. Unfortunately, I don't have the linguistic skills to discuss this with Seb, so these thoughts just go around and around in my head as I care for Dylan and wonder about his future.

Aside from breastfeeding and pregnancy hormones, physically, my body has been completely healed by the doctor, no stretch marks, no nothing. Actually, I think I look better than before because my breasts are gigantic now filled with milk, which makes me look even thinner. I'm still a bit overweight from the pregnancy. I was so hungry, and everyone loved feeding me, but I'm sure I will lose that weight too.

Seb takes good care of himself, and he sees me as an extension of him. My only hope is that when it's time, he exercises me with lots of sex and not hitting the gym or whatever he does.

At the moment, Seb isn't worried about my weight because he lets me eat human food every day as I complain that I'm so hungry from breastfeeding. Lately, I often think to myself, *I'd be completely happy if I wasn't his pet and if I knew what kind of future to expect.* But one thing I'm sure of, I love Dylan more than anyone I've ever loved before, and this love brings me contentment in this strange alien life that I've never felt before.

MONTHS PASS IN THIS LAZY, wonderful way, and I'm the happiest I've ever been in my life. One early morning, I'm feeding Dylan in our bed when Seb says before going on duty, "Today, we will rendezvous with a passenger ship."

He doesn't say anything more, and I don't know why or how that could affect me, so I just reply with a nod.

However, when Seb returns that afternoon with an Imperial woman in tow, I realize what he meant by telling me we were rendezvousing with a passenger ship. I quickly take Dylan out of his crib and run frantically into the bathroom. I say in broken Imperial language through my sobs, "You cannot take him. He's mine. He belongs with me. I'm his mother."

I don't know how to lock the bathroom door, so Seb easily opens it. I expect him to grab me and force Dylan out of my arms, but he doesn't. He just stands there patiently. He even looks a little sad.

"Ensley, he must go. He will be well taken care of. I promise. We cannot keep him here." He holds his grey hands out for Dylan.

I start to cry, an ugly cry. I hold my son tightly to my naked breast, "No, he needs me to eat." It's the only thing I can think of to logically keep him with me. I know that Imperial people like logic. And then another thought occurs to me, "I can go with him if he must go."

Seb points to the Imperial woman who entered with him, "This kind woman will be his nurse, and she will feed him and take care of all of his needs. Your weaning period with him is finished."

"When will I see him again?" I ask through my sobs still holding him to my breast.

"Never," Seb replies softly, and I almost see a bit of regret in his eyes. It's like he's seeing me for the first time, not as his pet but as his lover and the mother of his child.

"No," I push back against the stone wall. "You'll have to kill me first. I'm not giving him up."

Seb shakes his head at me, "Ensley, you must let go, or you will hurt him. I promise you he will have a good life. He will never know his mother was a pet. I will make sure he has a good Imperial life."

I start crying uncontrollably at his nasty words. I'm so hurt, his words, 'He will never know his mother was a pet' cut me like a knife and now it isn't difficult for Seb to take the baby from me with just a bit of force.

He hands Dylan off to the woman who disappears with it. I can't move for a few seconds. I crumble down and cry on the cold bathroom floor. I don't care if I die right then. A few seconds later, my anger takes over. I swiftly rise through my tears and bolt for the door, past Seb before he can grab me and down the hallway. I can hear Dylan crying, and I follow the sound of his wailing. *My baby is crying for me.* I run so fast because I'm so upset, "I'm coming for you. Mommy is coming. They won't take you from me."

Seb runs after me, and I hear an alarm go off. Purple lights start flashing everywhere, accompanied by a loud siren. Before I can reach Dylan, some of the crew catch me and hold me back. I scream and punch at them, but they hold me tightly. I sob and scream in Imperial, "No, it's my baby! I'm his mother. He needs me!" as I watch the Imperial woman quickly turn the corner out of sight. It isn't long before I can no longer hear Dylan's cries.

I continue to fight while all these grey alien men, familiar faces, look down at me and easily hold me down. "I hate you all. Do you hear me? I hate you." I say it in English, and they all just give me surprised and pitying looks. I expect them to manhandle me up and take me back to Seb's quarters, but none of them do. They just stare at me, holding me tight enough to keep me in place but not enough to hurt me. They are all looking at me as if it's a shock that I'd feel this way about being separating from my child.

Within seconds, Seb comes and gently picks me up and carries me back to his quarters.

He puts me on the bed.

I can't stop sobbing.

Seb kneels before me, "He is going to have a good life, Ensley." He brushes my tears off my face with his large thumbs, "Why are you so upset?"

I look at him in disbelief, and not being able to control my hand, I slap him hard across the face.

Seb is more surprised than angry. After he gets over his initial shock at what I've done, he stands and turns away from me.

I watch him, expecting him to turn around and punish me, but he doesn't, and when he does turn to answer the doorbell that chimes a second later, I see that he has had tears in his eyes. I don't know why, but that makes me feel better. That I hurt him today too. Then a thought crosses my mind, *That maybe he didn't want Dylan to go either.*

But even if that is true, for me, I need to blame Seb for this. I need to be angry with someone specifically, and I chose him. I can't accept that I just gave Dylan away. That I let him be taken from me and I'm still alive. I'm a terrible mother and I can't help but think, *I deserve to be a pet.*

The doctor comes in, and Seb explains that I'm devastated at seeing my baby leave the ship.

I just sit there on the bed, shooting Seb the nastiest looks I can while the doctor comes over to me.

Seb responds by just looking at me without any emotion whatsoever.

I want him to be nasty back, but he isn't, and that makes me angry too.

The doctor tries to pat my head, and I back away and say in Imperial, "Don't touch me."

The doctor is clearly surprised by my outburst, but gets control of himself quickly, and responds calmly, "Ensley, poor Ensley. Let me help you."

I surprise myself by just crying more and allowing the doctor to hold a device over me, but all the time saying again and again, "I don't want to feel better. I want to feel this pain. This pain is for my baby, who you all just took from me. You took my baby."

Seb and the doctor are both looking at me as if I'm crazy, which suits me just fine because I feel insane.

I hurt so much for my baby, and I don't want to relieve this pain. I wasn't strong enough to keep him.

"This is going to make you feel better and help you sleep," the doctor says, before I fall asleep.

My last words are, "I deserve this pain."

IN THE NEXT days and weeks, I don't want to do anything. The young man has to fight to go for walks or get me in the shower. But no one punishes me. No one pets me. I wear what Seb calls my settling-in clothing, and no one stops me. It's as if the entire crew is mourning with me for the loss of Dylan, and it's the only thing that keeps me from ultimately going crazy.

I try to sleep in my own bed because I hate Seb for sending our child away, but he won't let me. He says I shouldn't face this sadness alone. I want to ask him if he's terribly sad too, but I'm too angry to allow him that emotion. Although I suspect he must be and that he actually might need me as much as I need him. I presume that my being sad about the loss of Dylan only makes him confront his own emotions about it, which he obviously finds uncomfortable.

Thankfully, Seb has not tried to touch me sexually since Dylan left. Otherwise, I might kill him in his sleep. He has told me over and over again that Dylan is safe and will have a good life, but there's so much more I want to know, but I don't have the Imperial words to understand everything Seb says. I hate that I don't know what's happened. I try to console myself that ignorance is bliss, but I worry because I'm sure Seb thinks I have a great life too, but I don't want Dylan to be a pet nor a second-class citizen being raised by Imperial people who will discriminate against him. I've never been religious, but when Seb goes to make his own prayers in the shrine I pray as well to his Imperial gods that Dylan will not be a pet, but an equal man like Seb.

* * *

Seb

I THINK the experts on humans are wrong. Ensley was like a rabid beast when our son was taken from her. Even now, after weeks have passed, she is still not herself. She cries all the time and is miserable.

Every day, I remind Ensley that our son will have a good life. Every day, I must reassure her that he will not be a pet, but she doesn't believe me. I want to explain that he has been taken back to the Imperial homeworld to be raised in my household as my son. It's true he can never join the military, but there are many other useful jobs he can have in the Empire. If he ever asks me, I will not feel ashamed to tell him about Ensley nor how she uncharacteristically fought to keep him with her. How much she loves him. I think that is something I would want to know about my mother. My son, who I named Tema, will be raised with the awareness that he couldn't stay here on ship because he will be raised Imperial. I don't think he will hold too much against me for separating him from his mother, nor that she is human. None of her barbaric traits would have been passed to him, only her clean genes and he will be prized when it's time for him to take an Imperial wife.

After Ensley's reaction to Tema's departure, I resolutely believe humans are more evolved then we give them credit for. Ensley cares for her baby just as much as an Imperial woman would. When the day arrived to say 'goodbye' to Tema, I was already feeling sad about having to send him away, and I was looking to Ensley for emotional support as I thought it would be easier for her as a human to simply say 'goodbye.' But, when she ran after him frantically, I had to take a moment not to breakdown from my own grief before chasing after her. No one ever mentioned having a human would be so emotionally difficult.

I see Ensley differently now and so does the crew. No one expected her to fight for her child like an Imperial woman, and because she did, we can no longer see her as a pet. But what she is now, I do not know. I feel it's wrong to keep her as a pet, but what can I do? I bought her and forced her into this role. She is my responsibility, I cannot let her go freely in the galaxy, she will just be abducted and then sold again as pet. I cannot return her to Earth as it is off-limits. I cannot acknowledge her as not a pet or I will be stripped of my command and put into a mental institution. But there is an unspoken and uncomfortable knowingness between the crew and myself, *Ensley is not a pet and we have used her terribly.*

Now we are making an unnecessary stop at Kopio station just for Ensley. We will stay here for a few days. I have lied to Imperial command and told them the stop is so that we can replace power conduits that are difficult to print, but the truth is, there's a human expert here and lots of other humans for Ensley to play with. I think it will do her well to see the human expert and play with other humans. Maybe they can offer her the comfort that I cannot.

When we arrive at the station, I dress Ensley in her settling-in clothing. I know she doesn't want anyone petting her or seeing her body. We don't even discuss it anymore.

I put on her leash, for show, and lead her out into the massive station. I follow the signs to the human expert with whom I've made an appointment. When we arrive at the expert's office, there's a sizable human play area. I look at Ensley, but she doesn't even seem interested in joining the other humans, so I don't even ask if she wants to. I check-in with reception and take a seat, Ensley sits quietly at my feet.

After more than a few minutes, it's our turn. I lead Ensley into the office and I'm not surprised the pet expert has her own human pet there. I sit down, and again Ensley sits at my feet.

"Captain, how can I help you today?" the pet expert asks, eyeing Ensley quizzically.

I explain everything that has happened with Ensley from the beginning, and I'm also quick to point out that she's not stupid or mentally ill, that this depression she's currently suffering from is just a temporary state. My greatest fear in coming here is that it's recommended that Ensley is put down because she showed great affection for her offspring.

The expert listens to me patiently and then asks her human to talk to Ensley, "Ask her why she is sad in human."

The other human comes forward, she has skin the color of the fertile earth on my homeworld, and it's flawless. She reminds me of one of the other pets that were in the cage with Ensley when I bought her, and I wonder for a minute if she is the same. I look at Ensley, but she doesn't give any indication of knowing the other pet, so I assume she is not. I've not seen enough humans to really tell them apart. When she speaks, she has the most melodic voice, although I have no idea what she is saying, and Ensley doesn't look up at her.

Time passes, and the human touches Ensley's shoulder as she continues to talk to her.

Ensley looks up and starts talking in her human language in a such a rush of words, I can hardly believe it. I hear my name more than a few times, and it doesn't sound like I'm being spoken about well.

Finally, the other human reports, "She's upset that her child was taken away from her, and she worries that he will have a terrible life without her. She worries he will be a prostitute pet like her."

"Explain the custom of hybrid children," the expert says to the human, and she nods.

Ensley replies to the translation, but the other human doesn't translate.

"What did she say?" I ask impatiently.

The other human struggles for what to say and finally decides on, "I couldn't make out what she meant. Her language is not my mother tongue."

"Fine," says the expert letting it go. "Tell her that all her children will be well-cared for and have a better life than she could ever give them either as a pet or as a mother on Earth."

The other human tells Ensley, and she says nothing, but I can see from the expression on her face; those explanations don't make her feel content about the situation.

I address the human expert's pet myself, "Tell her our son is with my family. He is being raised as any Imperial boy would be except that he will not be allowed to join the military. Tell her that even if she was Imperial, our son would still be there. Explain that children are not allowed on warships." I want to also add, 'Tell her I miss him too,' but I would be locked away in a mental institution if I said such a thing to my pet about our offspring.

The human tells Ensley, and for the first time in a long time, she looks at me with some warmth to her eyes. I feel relieved, even if it is a small thing, it is a step towards repairing our relationship, which must be mended. I am not going to give Ensley up. She is mine, and no matter how sad she is, I am going to provide for her the best care I can for the rest of her life. She is, for better or worse, my responsibility.

Ensley looks directly into my eyes, her green eyes full of hope, and asks in Imperial, "Can I see our son?"

"I can show you videos and images from the homeworld."

"Why can't I really see him?"

It hurts me to see the sadness in her eyes, but before I can answer her, the pet expert says sharply, "Because you are a pet, Ensley."

Ensley moves so quickly I barely have time to grab her leash. She lunges at the pet expert, trying to attack her, "Ensley, no." I hold her close to my chest while I apologize to the expert. Then I ask, "Is there any way I could get a translation chip for her?"

"We have got a prototype. It only has a 50% success rate. If it doesn't work, you don't get your UCs back. I wouldn't recommend it. She's not stupid, just badly behaved and that's your fault for not training her better, Captain. I'd recommend you watch my videos and start over from the very beginning. You need to be a better owner. More punishments, not a translation chip."

I am annoyed, but I want to know more about the translation chip, so I control my urge to tell the pet expert that I think she's an idiot and instead ask, "When could she get the translation chip?"

The expert checks her schedule on her 3D computer, "Tomorrow morning at seven, and then I would need to monitor for a few hours afterward. The whole procedure costs about 2,000 UC. Are you sure you want to waste that kind of money on your pet? I know you're a well-respected Captain, but even for you, that must be a lot of UCs."

I don't hesitate, "Yes. I'm certain I want to do it." As I walk out with Ensley still in my arms, I say, "I'll see you tomorrow morning."

The expert nods, and her human says something to which Ensley replies to in the human language. Once we are outside the door and out of earshot of the expert, I set Ensley down, "I know that woman wasn't nice, but she's going to give you a translator. I think that would help a lot. I don't know how much you understand, but I'd never do anything cruel to our child or to you." I brush her yellow hair back from her face, "I feel there are too many miscommunications between us." As I look into her eyes, I doubt she even understands my last comment, but I need to say it, if only for my own peace of mind.

Ensley nods anyway, and I realize that I want so much more from her. I want to know what she really needs to bring her peace. I hope that I won't be disappointed with the translation chip. I hope that it works and that when we can understand each other, she will have thoughts just as deep and clear as any Imperial person and that I will not be mistaken in that I now believe humans are not the wild beasts we think they are.

I point to the play area, "Would you like to go?"

"Yes."

I lead her to the play area. It is very colorful with lots of balls, a swimming area, and human food. I take Ensley's leash off and pay the fee for her to go in. Then I stand outside the transparent force field, watching my human interact with the other pets. As always, my Ensley is hesitant about approaching different groups, and it takes her a few tries to find someone to play with, but soon she seems to find another female pet, and they sit with their feet in the pool talking. I make eye contact with Ensley and wave that I will be back soon. I know that even if she wants to leave before I return, her Imperial is good enough that she can communicate that to the guards.

She nods.

Then I decide to go have a drink. Finding out that all this time, Ensley thought I had done something horrible to our son was emotionally draining. I don't think she hates me, but it never occurred to me that she thought I could ever do something so cruel as to make Tema a pet or whatever else she imagined.

I walk into a nearby bar and order a drink. The man to my left addresses me, "You have a pet, Captain?"

"How did you guess?"

"You have the look of a man who has a pet," he smiles. "And I saw you walking with her before. And this is the closest bar to the human play area, I think we all have pets. That's why we are all drinking."

"How long have you had yours?" I ask.

"More than ten years."

"Long time. I've only had mine for about an Imperial year."

"It's always difficult in the beginning."

"I'm glad to hear that," I admit, "The human-pet expert made me feel like it was my fault my pet was so miserable."

"Oh, I saw that woman once, a nasty piece of work. Let me guess, your pet was upset you sent your first offspring back to the homeworld."

I look at him in astonishment. I thought Ensley was the only one. Now I'm even more sure that humans are not really pets.

"Look, I've got ten years on you. Most of the information from so-called pet experts is wrong. Humans love their offspring just as much as we do. They learn and feel just like we do, but by the time we figure all this out, we've already bought them. If we mention this to anyone, we will lose our positions or worse, so we are caught in the pet limbo, as I call it."

"I'm beginning to see that."

"Now, my Mira is much more accepting of the practice, especially since the law might change soon."

"That's just an IGC fantasy, it'll never change."

"I don't think so. Humans just set up their first station on their sister planet called 'Mars.' If they last the year, then the law outlawing humans as pets will go into effect."

"Humans don't have the technology or the physical strength to get off their planet for more than an IGC year. It won't happen," even though I say the words confidently, I hadn't been monitoring what the humans were doing in these past months. I had been too concerned with other things in my life. Too emotionally drained to even consider the unlikely possibility that humans might be accepted into the IGC, an organization they didn't even know about yet.

"The humans are almost at the halfway point. You should start to consider it as a real possibility and make plans."

"But what would we all do? Our pets have no place in Imperial society. Where would they go?"

"I don't know. Mira, my pet, says that she would like to be returned to Earth. But it would be difficult for me as I've grown so fond of having her around."

"Would you really do that? Return her? It's illegal to enter the Solar System as humans call it," I say, and then we both laugh because it is ridiculous humans had not renamed their system when they found out they were not the only ones with a solar system.

"Well, if they manage this colony on Mars, it won't be forbidden anymore, and I could visit her sometimes, I guess, as long as the humans accepted the terms of the IGC," the man says a bit sadly. "It will all be so different. But one thing is for sure, if humans accomplish this, then they can no longer be our pets."

"I don't think it'll happen. What would the humans on Earth think if thousands of pets just showed up again? How embarrassing to say they had been taken as pets and lived that way?"

The man shrugs, "Hopefully, you are right, the humans will fail, and we will never need to think about this."

We both drink side-by-side in silence.

I am lost in my own thoughts. I think about the translation chip and wonder if it will work tomorrow, but odds aren't great, and this will wipe out a good chunk of my savings, but I owe it to Ensley.

After I finish two drinks, I take my leave of my drinking companion and walk past the human play area to check on Ensley. I walk up to the transparent force field and see her, still talking to the same human with her feet in the water. She looks content so I decide to allow her to stay as long as she likes. I talk to the assistant and have him give Ensley a communication bracelet.

I watch him put it on her and explain to her how it works. I motion for her to press it when she wants to go.

She nods at me.

When the attendant comes back, I transfer him UCs, "Make sure nothing happens to her."

"Of course, not Captain. She will be safe and happy to play as long as she likes. We never close here on Kopio station."

Satisfied, I turn and leave. I walk around through the station, not really needing anything in particular. Kopio station is massive and is a natural meeting point for aliens from all over the galaxy. I don't know why, but I walk into the slave market section of the station. I pass a lot of slaves, all of lesser species in cages. They don't bother to rise when I walk by because Imperial people don't buy slaves.

As I reach the end of this particular slave market, surprisingly, I pass a small cage and see a human inside.

I stop and inquire with the slave master. "You do know, it is illegal for humans to be slaves under IGC law?"

"The way I see it," says the slave master, "The IGC law will be changed in half a year, and then, humans will be open game for slavery. All of you," he points his finger at my chest, "will have to give up your precious pets, and then every other slave trader and I will be waiting to sell them as they should be. Humans aren't pets; they are meant to be slaves. They are just as clever as you or me, just weak and undeveloped. Now what are you going to do? Turn me into the IGC?"

I want to tell him that he is wrong, but I know in my heart he isn't and who would be a better judge of lesser species than a slave trader?

"Would you like to buy this one? Just to keep for half a year? I'll give you a discount. But I have to warn you, she cries all the time. She's good for a rut, though."

I instinctively look at the woman, she is older than Ensley with dark hair and just sits looking at me with a dead expression. I feel sorry for her, and I wonder if we are wrong, not elevating humans higher, offering them some kind of protection. They are as genetically close to Imperial people as any other species can be, and that should mean something, shouldn't it? That maybe we have been mistaken, thinking they are so much less than us just because they are so technologically inferior, and their skin can be different colors.

"No, I already have a pet. Why don't you put her down if she's is such a bother?" I look at the old human and wish I had the UCs to buy her to put her out of her misery myself.

"Oh, because there will be an Imperial sucker who comes along sooner or later and wants her. Or an Octopod, you know what they like to do with human women as their pets."

I give him a disgusted look. Everyone knew what Octopods liked to do with human women. I had seen it once in a video, and the terrible images still haunted me. I only hoped after seeing that video that the human woman in it hadn't lived very long afterward. The galaxy is a brutal place, especially for inferior species. Humans are so beautiful but so ignorant and easy to abduct.

I want to punch the slave trader in front of me for even suggesting he would sell this human to an Octopod, but instead, I just ignore his comment and walk on thinking, *I cannot save every human, but I can protect my human.*

AFTER A FEW HOURS, I am notified on my IC that Ensley wants to be picked up. I go back to the pet play area, and when she sees me, she gives the other human woman a hug and then comes to the door eagerly and waits for me to put her leash on.

"Are you hungry?"

"I ate human food in there." She hesitates and then says, "Seb?"

She hardly ever speaks to me anymore, so I stop walking and look down at her concerned face, "What?"

"I want different clothes. Clothes I choose."

I don't know what to say, "You don't like what I have bought you?"

"Sometimes I want to wear something for myself."

I resist the urge to pat her head, "Okay, but not all the time."

I start walking her to the nearest clothing stores for human pets. There are three in a row, "Which one do you want to go to?"

She points to the largest one.

We are greeted by a shop assistant and her pet. Her pet starts to speak to Ensley but then very quickly tells me, "I don't speak your pet's language. I'll find another who does," and disappears.

Ensley starts looking at clothing, and I explain to the shop assistant that I am letting her choose.

The shop assistant gives me a funny look, but before she can ask me why I am letting my pet chose her own clothing, another pet comes over and starts chatting away to Ensley and Ensley seems very happy to talk.

"She wants more conservative clothing," the other pet says and then starts leading Ensley around and showing her things. "She doesn't like all the men on your ship touching her. She says it's fine when you touch her sometimes, but not them."

I didn't think Ensley would want to be covered as the most beautiful thing about humans is their fur. I ask the shop assistant's pet, "Is this normal for humans? To not want attention in this way?"

The shop assistant interrupts before the other human pet can answer me, "You know they are all different, maybe your pet is just a little weird, Captain."

I look at the shop assistant with dismay and then ask the other pet again, adding, "I want to hear her answer."

"Taking advice from a pet? I would say you are one step away from losing your mind," the shop assistant scolded me.

I ignore the shop assistant and look at her pet, waiting for an answer.

"No, on Earth, we stay with one man usually, and we cover ourselves with clothing."

"Truly?" I can't believe it. I look at the pet, trying to decide if she is lying or not.

She nods and then chases after Ensley who has wandered off to look at more clothing, probably fearing punishment from the sales assistant for answering me.

"Don't punish her, I only wanted to know what she thought as ridiculous as it might be."

The sales assistant gives me another funny look, "I think you've become too close with your pet; you should sell her. There is a slave trader who has some humans on the station, maybe you can trade her for another one?"

I frown, "No, I think I will just try to make this one better."

"You're not doing a good job letting her choose her own clothing."

I ignore the sales assistant and follow Ensley and the other human back to the fitting rooms.

Ensley tries on some clothing that covers most of her body.

"Is that what you want?" I ask disbelievingly.

"Yes, I want this," she runs her small hands down her hips over the fabric, visibly enjoying the feel of it.

"No one can see your fur. Your beauty," I softly protest.

Ensley looks at me without speaking for a few seconds in the reflection of the mirror, "Not all the time, but sometimes, I want this."

I nod acquiescence, and the shop assistant tailors the clothes to fit Ensley's body perfectly.

I pay the UCs for the clothing and allow her to wear some of it out of the shop and have the rest sent to the ship.

It occurs to me then that Ensley must be very tired as she has been out for a lot of the day without a nap, I decide to take her back to the ship. She insists that she can walk, but I won't let her. I pick her up and carry her. She weighs almost nothing, and with everything that I have learned today, I want to hold her. I don't know whether or not I should believe everything, but even if some of it is true, I feel guilty. And I have no way to express this guilt to her, so I hold her close to me. When we return to my quarters, I take off her clothes and put her into my bed. She doesn't smile at me as she used to before Tema was born, but I don't feel the hatred she had for me yesterday either, and this pleases me. The stop to Kopio station has not been in vain, even if the translation device is a failure tomorrow.

THE NEXT MORNING, we go back to the human expert's office for the translation chip procedure. I let Ensley wear her new clothing of her choosing. This seems to make her happy even though everyone else assumes that her body must be scarred or deformed in a way for me to dress her like this inside the station. I only add to their assumptions as she is also wearing the jewelry, I bought her as well. I thought she looked too plain in her conservative clothing. I brought out the jewelry and asked her if she wanted to wear it. I was surprised and pleased that she said 'yes.'

When we arrive at the human-pet expert's office, we are ushered in, and I remove Ensley's leash.

"Please get on the medical bed," the expert says to Ensley and then to me, "You can wait outside."

The last thing that I want to do is wait outside and leave Ensley alone with this bitter woman, "I'll stay if it's all the same to you," I say this in a way that makes it perfectly clear that I am not leaving Ensley's side.

The expert shrugs her shoulders and then goes about her work.

I silently pray to the gods as I watch the expert and her nurse hover over Ensley with medical computers and devices. I look at the computer readouts above their heads of Ensley's brain, but I'm not a doctor, I don't know what any of it means.

I'm concerned though, my own doctor said she might become brain-damaged from this kind of procedure. So I watch and try to remain clam.

After 15 minutes, the procedure seems to have worked. The human-pet expert says to Ensley, "If I told you that all the faith the man had had had had no effect on the outcome of his life. Would you say he had a lot of faith?"

Ensley shook her head, "He had not a lot of faith."

"Correct."

"Strange sentence to ask," I comment. Clearly not understanding why a doctor would ask such a thing.

"It's a linguistically difficult question that there's no way she could have understood without a translator."

"And now for you, Captain, please come lie down. It'll only take a second. We just need to add her language to your current chip, and then we have it."

"Ensley speak to the Captain in your human language," the human expert commands after a few minutes.

Ensley looks at me and says so clearly and without a trace of an accent, "My name is Ensley. I come from Earth, and I always want to wear clothing like this." She looks down at her clothing and then back up at me, her green eyes shining with the realization I can understand her clearly for the first time.

I sit up from the medical bed and say, "We will discuss it later." I am ecstatic that the procedure has worked. I thank the human expert while we prepare to leave.

"No need to thank me, Captain, you paid enough UCs already. Just don't mention it to too many people. Until the new law is passed, this is still somewhat illegal, you know, it's quite a grey area whether humans should be allowed translators." The pet expert looks at Ensley then, "You must turn the translator on and off to reply in the Imperial language, if you don't, everyone else will only hear you speaking your human language, and if you try to speak the Imperial language with your translator on, you won't be able to hear yourself, only your human language, do you understand?"

Ensley nods happily, "I understand."

When we are back on the ship, as we both need to lay down, especially Ensley as embedded translators are known for bad headaches, especially dodgy ones. Ensley asks me, "What did the woman mean when she said, by law this is still illegal for a little while longer?"

"The IGC will enforce a law forbidding humans to be Imperial pets if humans succeed in their new colony on one of your nearby planets."

"What's the IGC?"

"It's a loose governing body of all of the galactic civilizations with a technology level above five."

"Humanity is level four?"

"Yes. You have been level 4 for a long time. All you need to do to reach level 5 is set up a colony and survive for one IGC year somewhere other than your home planet. You've had the technology but lacked the cooperativeness for a long time."

"We aren't good at working together," Ensley replies. "This planet, I assume you mean Mars?"

"Yes, I think so. I can't remember the exact name of your sister planet," I admit. "Don't worry, it'll never happen." Before she can answer I interrupt her, "Ensley, I want to tell you that I am sorry I bought you. I didn't know you could think. I didn't know you weren't a pet."

It seems like an eternity before she answers me. Her face is unreadable to me.

"I know you didn't know. And for a long time, I thought I could be your pet..." she trailed off and tears silently began falling from her eyes.

I wipe her tears away, "Until Tema," I say.

"How could you give away our baby?" she asks me for the millionth time, but now it sounds so real to me. I am hearing it in perfect Imperial for the first time, and I feel more guilty than I ever have before. I take her into my arms, and I'm pleased she allows it. I stroke her back and say, "It's the Imperial way. I was told by human pet experts that you wouldn't mind or remember after a few days. I should have known better, even before that you showed signs of being more clever than what I had been told. I'm sorry Ensley."

Ensley just cries into my shoulder as I hold her and tell her what I have been telling her for weeks now, "He's going to have a good life. He's safe."

"How do I know that?" she asks into my shoulder. "I've never been to your homeworld. How do I know how they would treat him? I worry he will be discriminated against. What if someone finds out I'm his mother?"

I run my hands through her hair, "You must trust me." I am wary to explain everything to her because it's just occurred to me that the Empire has known all along that humans weren't really pets but this was a convenient way to use them to keep our gene pool diverse without having to offer anything to humans.

"Have you received any pictures or videos of him?"

"No, but if I ask they will be sent."

She leans back and slaps me, "You could have asked all this time and you didn't?"

I grab her hand before she hits me again, "I have had written reports. He is a baby. You know he just lies there. He is healthy." She shakes her hand and I release it.

Ensley points to the sitting room, "Go and request everything now."

I get out of bed and do it. I send a message to Tema's nanny. Then I return to bed, "She will send something as soon as she can I'm sure and then I will show you."

"I want something sent every day."

"You understand you cannot go to the homeworld and we cannot have him here, right?"

"I'm not stupid Seb. I just couldn't communicate with you before because I didn't have the translator."

"I know," I admit. Then we just lay side-by-side in silence until Ensley asks me another question.

"What would you do if humans did join the IGC and I was no longer your pet?"

"I don't know. I met a slave trader on the station who said that you all would become slaves. Well, that's what he and his ilk would like to see, anyway."

"You would sell me to a slave trader?" she sits up quickly, horrified by the idea.

"No, no. Never," I lie, I don't want to tell her that I might be forced to do it, but that I would make sure she would go to a good master like a Yuksen who keep slaves to merely listen to them recite poetry and sing songs.

"What would you do then?"

"I don't know."

"Could you take me back to Earth?"

"Possibly, it would be difficult."

"But it would be the right thing to do, to return me to Earth. I don't want to be a slave. Being a pet is bad enough."

I look at her in shock then. I take her in my arms and look into her green eyes, "You're not happy being a pet? I provide everything for you, and I adore you." I run my fingers through her long yellow hair.

"In a different galaxy Seb, maybe you and I would be something different to one another, but I don't know if I want to be a pet. I had a life on Earth before I was taken. I had things that I always thought I would do."

I feel incredibly guilty. So guilty in fact, I don't even want to hear what her future aspirations were before she was abducted. But as part of my punishment I must hear it, "Tell me about what could have been if Mikeal had not picked you up."

"Who's Mikeal?"

"One of the green aliens called Dulus who abducted you," I reply evenly.

She hesitates only for a second before deciding to let that go and answer my question, "I used to dream that I would get promoted at work and actually buy an apartment in the city. That I meet a man to marry and have a child with him…" she trailed off and I can feel her tears on my shoulder.

"I'm sorry you were taken away from all of that Ensley."

She shakes her head, "I'm lucky you bought me. You should have seen what came in before you."

"I can imagine." I hold her close, "But you're human. This must be a much better life than you could have ever had on Earth."

"Possibly," she tries to squirm away from me, from my words, but I hold her fast.

"Talk to me," I command her quietly.

"Look at us, the only difference is the color of our skin. We are the same. Name real things that make you better than humans besides being more technologically advanced?"

I think about her question, and I reply honestly, "I can think of nothing but look at the way your species behaves, not like us. Not civilized. Even when I first saw you, you were fighting with the other human women in your cage over nothing, and one of those humans even urinated all over my leg. How is that civilized?"

She replies with a crazed laugh, "You think this is civilized? You are barbarians. You parade me around naked and touch me in places you would never touch an Imperial woman. You allow your men to use my body for their own lustful desires. You take away my son without even telling me what is going to happen to him. That's anything but civilized, Seb. It's cruel, and I hate it."

I'm indignant, but I don't want her to stop talking.

"You send your babies away to be cared for by someone else. You have rape orgies,"

I interrupt her there, "Do you feel I raped you?"

"You're kidding, right?"

"No, tell me. Do you think I raped you?" I am aghast at the thought that she thought I might have raped her.

"Not really, but all this so-called human-pet training is degrading," she throws her hands up and continues talking. I stopped listening for a minute, relieved that she didn't think I raped her.

"Stop there, this just proves how backward humanity is that you don't view these things as 'civilized,'" I counter.

"No, you don't understand," she has a cute pout on her lips. I have only seen a couple times before, and I can't help but lean up and kiss her.

She doesn't pull away.

I pull away and whisper in her ear, "Ensley, I can't say sorry enough to undo what I've done. I'm sorry there was so much you didn't and don't understand, but you mean more to me than any woman I've ever known, and I will not call you my pet in private if you don't want to be my pet. But," I put both of my hands on her face while looking into her human eyes on the brink of tears, "We will always be together. We must make this work."

She doesn't speak but kisses me back then.

We have never kissed before this moment, and I am shattered. I feel so much for this human woman. I want things I never imagined I would want from her. My hands start to roam her body as if it is the first time I am touching her warm skin. "I love the feel of your soft body next to mine," I run my hands up and down her torso and thighs. "I love your fur," I gently trace my fingers through over her sex. "And," I kiss her neck then her face, "I don't ever want to part from you. Tell me what you want."

Her body is reacting to me, but I want her mind too. I feel this is the moment she is going to believe me that I meant her no ill-will and forgive me if that is even possible for her.

"Ensley," I say against her neck while I kiss her lightly, "what can I do for you?"

"Seb," she breaths my name heavily. "I want you to have hard sex."

I laugh, remembering how I punished her that before, "You don't know what that really means in Imperial. What you said before is close but not what you've said now."

"What's the difference?" she asked between kisses, "You were so angry."

"You were asking for me to purposely have sex with you so strongly that I would bruise your cervix."

Ensley stopped kissing me and looked into my eyes, "How is that even a thing? And you call yourselves civilized."

I shrug, "It's depraved but some people like that kind of thing..." I trail off, I don't know why I even explained. I just want my Ensley now.

"Call me 'your little pet'," she tells me.

"What?" I'm so confused. I thought she wanted to drop all pretenses when we were alone.

"Please, I love it when you call me that. It's so wicked."

I am overjoyed by her words, and I don't need to be told twice, "Come here, my naughty little pet."

MONTHS PASS. Ensley no longer wants my squire to attend to her or take her on walks. I allow her to roam free in the ship, within reason.

Ensley asks me for more freedom every week. Yesterday after I finished a video call with my housekeeper on my homeworld she asked me if she could contact her family on Earth.

"Do they have the technology to receive such a call?" I asked her.

She shook her head, "I don't think so. Not like this. But we have something like messages. Maybe if I was able to look around on your computer you could help me?"

Of course, I feel sorry for Ensley, but I must put limitations on her freedoms and expectations, "Please just accept this is your future and stop looking to the past."

She nods.

I knew this only meant that she would soon think of another way to ask me the same thing. I had come to realize that Ensley was a fighter in every way. I found it curious and questioned if this was why humans never seemed to get their act together as a species. If they all functioned like Ensley there would only be moments of compromises but no long-term effects and therefore no long-term progress. Ensley and I would compromise but she rarely held to her end of the bargain for long, she would always find a loophole to do what she wanted. I found it charming in her as she was still under my control, but it's easy to see how detrimental it would be to an entire species.

TODAY I NEED to return to my quarters while on duty. As I walk in, I am disappointed Ensley is out, probably walking around the ship with my squire. They spent countless hours together before so it's not uncommon that they still walk together now, but Ensley without her leash.

I walk over and pick up some of her discarded clothing from the floor. I would never understand why she liked to try on different clothing before making a choice. I put the clothing neatly back in the wardrobe.

I wonder briefly, *What am I doing living this way with my human?* But then I remind myself, that I don't care anymore. My entire life I have followed the rules of my society and done everything correctly. Still my wife died prematurely, and I was assigned the most boring post out of all my counterparts from the academy. Ensley is the one thing in my life that is real. That makes me feel alive and I wasn't going start wasting my time asking myself if living like this with her was right. It was right for me and right for her too.

However, this change has not been easy for either of us. As Ensley learns more about the galaxy and Imperial culture, she begins to ask me for things she cannot have. She never tires of asking to see our son Tema and asking to speak to him herself. I've told her a hundred times that is out of the question. I know that she will always love her child, our child and it's why I know I was wrong in making her my pet. But she has no proper place here. She isn't a pet, she's not my wife nor is she a prostitute. She is just human Ensley.

THAT EVENING, Ensley asked me about identification necklaces. I told her that we all wear identification jewelry in the Empire, so we always know who other people are without asking. I show her mine, "I know you can't read it, but it says my name and rank."

She laughs at me, "That's the opposite of pets on Earth, we give them jewelry, so everyone knows who they belong to."

"Humans, always getting it wrong," I comment casually from my desk.

After a few minutes of silence, Ensley says, "I want an Imperial necklace. Am I not a part of the Empire? Your squire told me that even slaves have them."

I stop working and turn to her, "This is true, but as I have to remind you, for all intents and purposes, you are still a pet. You have no status in the Empire. No one would ever have a reason to speak to you about anything of importance."

Ensley frowns, "I wish things were different."

"They aren't," I say matter-of-factly and return to what I'm doing, hoping she will drop this conversation. Suddenly I feel Ensley put her head on my lap, the way she used to do, before Tema was born. I put my hand on her head and say softly, "This life is what it is. I'm not important enough to change anything."

"I know," she says sadly.

"I'm not sorry I bought you. You would have been sold to another alien and we would have never been together."

"Do you think I'll go to the Afterworld with you?"

I stop stroking her head, "I've never thought about it."

"I've thought about it ever since you brought me here. You know you pray a lot?"

"I don't think so, once a day…" she interrupts me.

"Twice sometimes more. After Tema left, you prayed all the time. Your squire told me."

"I was worried about you. I needed direction."

"But what do you think? Will I be good enough to go to the Imperial afterword or will my spirit roam the galaxy forever?"

"I think you will go wherever humans go," I say honestly. I can see this angers her.

"Of course."

I can see her mind turning.

"Will you teach me to read?"

I look down at her horrified, "No Ensley."

"Remember that pet we met at the first station you took me to? She could read Imperial."

"She was old and worked in a shop and I'm sure she couldn't read very well. If someone found out you could read, what excuse could I give? You would be sent to a lab and dissected to discover if I had used some illegal medical procedure to enhance your brain."

"Who is going to tell? Not me."

"Ensley, no. Be content with this."

"I want to read. Maybe just to send some messages to some other pets. I get so bored just kicking my ball around all day."

I try not to look shocked, "You cannot send messages to other human pets. I would be arrested, my house broken up, and you would be put to death."

"I don't understand why it's such a big deal, I'm so bored."

I look at her seriously, I can't decide how much to tell her, "What if you led a pet revolt?"

Ensley looked blankly for a second, then burst out laughing, "A human-pet revolt? Ha. Be serious. Do I look like Spartacus to you?"

"I don't know who Spartacus is, but you are a human-pet and if you can read Imperial and use our technology you are a threat." I eye her and decide to leave it at that. I don't want to discuss my conspiracy theories with her. "Don't worry. I will always be here to take care of you."

"But what if you die?"

"My squire will take you."

Ensley makes a disgusted face, "He's a boy."

"He's a young man and it wouldn't be the same, per se, but that's who your new master would be if something were to happen to me. Or would you rather the doctor?"

"Your squire is fine," she answers quickly.

I smile, "I thought so. Now, stop all this nonsense. Look here, there's a pet convention on one of the Imperial homeworlds. Would you like to go? I could parade you around naked like these groomed human pets." I show Ensley pictures of the winning pets from last year.

"I wouldn't want my body to be on display like that. Would you look at all the hair on those humans. I don't look like that."

"No," I agreed. The winning pets were very furry. "And I wouldn't want the temptation to breed you for UCs afterward either." Something crossed her mind when I said that and I hoped she knew I wasn't serious. "Ensley?"

"It's nothing I was just remembering something. How about some chocolate?"

CHAPTER 7

Seb

"Captain," my first officer says and slides a screen over to me on the bridge.

I look at it and pale, "My office," I say and we both leave the bridge. Once inside I look at the announcement from the IGC more closely. It clearly states that humans have reached technology level 5 and will be offered membership. The announcement also specifically mentions human pets and say they must be set free.

"Captain?"

"I'm fine." I say, but I am anything but fine. My mind is racing. I don't want to lose Ensley.

"Maybe there's a way we could keep her here in secret? She could pretend to be a prostitute. We could change her skin color."

"How would we explain her human life sign every time we docked in Imperial space?"

"Maybe we could drop her off somewhere beforehand like Kopio station and then pick her up again?"

I shake my head, "We couldn't leave her alone on a station. She would be captured and sold into slavery within a day."

"What about the Yuksen? You could sell her to a good owner there?"

My face must have given away how I felt about that plan because he immediately backtracks.

"You could try to change the law and marry her, Captain."

"You know I don't have the UCs or the power to do something like that. Someone above me would have to do it and who is going to do that? If you are that rich and powerful you don't need to change the law."

My first officer agrees with me and we sit in silence.

Finally I say regretfully, "Find out what other people are doing. There are probably vessels returning to Earth to return pets," I can't bring myself to say, 'We will have to say "goodbye" to our beloved Ensley.'

My first officer nods.

"I will keep an eye out for the Empire wanting to change any of its laws regarding humans," I say. I don't want to say what I believe about the Empire just using humans to keep our gene pool healthy. But I do think if my suspicions are true, the Empire might try to strike up a formal agreement with Earth that maybe humans won't be pets, but rather wives or something along those lines.

My first officer leaves and I open my computer and begin searching. I sign myself up for every notification from the High Council and the Imperial Reproduction Agency with any news regarding humans. Then I begin to search human-pet experts advice on the current situation. They all seem to be holding the government line except for one.

I open a message to him.

I can't get through it's busy.

I look at his message again, it reads, "Petition the High Council to let humans stay as they are essential to our gene pool."

I try calling him again.

Busy.

I look for other human-pet experts who might say the same.

Nothing.

I try calling again and again.

I refresh his page a million times looking for a change.

Nothing.

Then after hours, his page and every record of that human-pet expert is removed.

I feel like I've lost my mind. I search for his name, it was a common Imperial name, lots of people appear but not this particular pet expert. I try again.

I put my head in my hands. I need to say 'goodbye' to my Ensley before something terrible happens. It's clear that the Empire doesn't want our secret about our relationship with humans to become public. But what's even more concerning to me is that I know my government isn't going to just give up using humans because the IGC has changed the law. I suddenly imagine Ensley and many other human pets being kept in large medical facilities for forced breeding purposes and I shudder.

I close my computer and begin making a list on my IC of all the things I need to prepare for Ensley's departure. Without a doubt, the Empire will want to show that human pets were returned to Earth. There will be at least one ship. No matter what the cost, I must put Ensley on it.

Just then there is a chime at my office door, "Enter."

My first officer enters, "Captain, there is only one cruiser returning to Earth and it's already sold out."

"Only one?"

"Yes," he opens a communal computer. "But there are rumors of second-hand tickets for a price. And our chance to rendezvous with it is in a few hours. We must act quickly."

"Of course," I say, "What's the rumored price?"

"Ten-thousand."

I look at the screen with the information of the ship. "I don't have that."

"I know," my first officer says sympathetically. "But I've already talked to some of the officers, and we agree this is the best for Ensley. If we combine our UCs we have enough."

I'm overwhelmed with emotion. I doubt anyone but the doctor

realizes the true implications of Ensley remaining out in the galaxy, but obviously they like her enough they would rather see her returned to Earth than become a slave. "I couldn't accept your UCs."

"That's going to be difficult because we already put them into your account. Buy Ensley a place back home before all the places are gone Captain."

My first officer brings up the second-hand tickets through the vessel's messaging page. He arranges it all and then looks at me expectantly, "We only need your fingerprint and voice activation."

My voice doesn't shake as I transfer the UCs, but I feel as if I had been hit with a hard blow to my stomach. When it is finished and I have a proof of receipt for her passage I say, "Thank you for this. I will thank the other officers personally as well after we send Ensley on her way."

"We all want to see her safe and we know you spent almost everything on her translator. But it was worth it. These last months of hearing her chatter, her jokes and her charm, we all know she is meant to go home. She has been a fleeting love affair for us all."

I can't answer my first officer. I'm too overwhelmed and don't trust myself to speak. I nod and dismiss him with my hand.

* * *

Ensley

"WHAT DO you mean the law has changed?" I ask Seb.

"Humans have managed to keep their colony alive on Earth's sister planet. There are two survivors after one IGC year and another ship on its way to help them and revive the settlement. IGC has been monitoring the transmissions."

"What does this mean?" I ask rhetorically. I know what this means, this has been on both of our minds for the last few months. Just when I felt like we had developed a relationship that worked for both of us. I was still Seb's pet in public, but I only had to wear my leash when we went off the ship. I'm closer to being his wife than a pet now. We talk, make love, and enjoy our time together. The last thing I want to do is leave. I love him. He is my everything.

"The IGC has given us one week to either make humans citizens of the Empire, which is impossible, as you know, we don't allow aliens to be citizens or we must set you free."

I interrupt him, "But what about those religious fanatics that say humans are some mythical tribe and that we are Imperial?"

Seb waves his hand away, "No one believes that. It's called a myth because that is exactly what it is. Humans and Imperial people are not the same species. It's just by chance we are so genetically similar."

"Will you set me free only to be taken as a slave then?"

"No, of course not, I'd sell you as a slave and make a profit," he says jokingly.

Over the months, since I have been able to talk to Seb, I began to appreciate his wicked sense of humor. "I'm serious. What are we going to do?"

"If I return you to my household in the Empire in secret, I'm afraid you will be killed by the other members of my house, and they might kill Tema too just to spite you. We've always kept pets and family separate."

"Charming family you have," I comment, but this information is nothing new to me.

We have discussed his family and obligations to them every time we watch a video or see an image of Dylan from the Imperial home-world. It makes me feel better during those times to know that Seb misses Dylan too. Although Imperial culture makes me uncomfortable, and I sometimes worry about our son, I look at Seb and some of the other men I have gotten to know onboard and think despite their culture having some bizarre and cruel customs, the few Imperial people that I know are overall decent people. It's the only thing that gives me hope that Dylan will turn out to be respectable too.

"I can't control my culture or people any more than you can your own," Seb replies seriously.

"I know, but the more I learn about your culture, the more I think some parts of it are wrong."

"I know you do," he says, casually running his fingers through my hair.

"Maybe you can get me a place on Falcon station. You know somewhere out of the way," I suggest.

"Until someone decides to take you as a slave," he replies.

"Maybe if there are enough of us who want to be free but remain in the galactic neighborhood, we can live in a group and hire guards to protect us," I suggest.

"No, there's only one option. You must return to Earth."

"No. We will find a way," I counter.

Seb shakes his head, "There's no safe place for humans out in the galaxy right now and there are worse things that can happen to you than being a slave." He pauses then deciding something, "Unless I'm going to become a pirate, I have to let you go. I wish things were different, that I could make them different, but we are only two small people in the galaxy. If I allow you to stay, the chance that you would stolen and sold into slavery is high."

I don't know when I started crying, but my face is wet and I say with some humor, "Well, at least the puppy pound won't pick me up again because I'm damaged goods now." I know he doesn't want me to go, and I don't want to leave him either. The thought of never seeing Seb or knowing anything about Dylan again breaks my heart, but I don't want to die at the end of an Octopod's tentacles either.

"Returning you to Earth is the only option, Ensley. I've booked you a place on a sizable Imperial passenger cruiser that has been commissioned to take human pets back to Earth. We will rendezvous with them in a just few hours. This is the only sanctioned Imperial ship returning human pets. All other pets will be released into the galaxy to fend for themselves."

"I guess I better not miss this chance then." I look up at him and can't help but step forward and put my arms around him. I say into his chest, "I will miss you so much." I know he doesn't like this extreme show of emotion, but I can't help it. I want him to say that he will miss me too, that he loves me, but I receive nothing except this physical contact.

Seb holds me for a good minute in silence. Then he lets go and opens his wardrobe. He takes out a black box. "Here is all of your jewelry. Silver is common on Earth too, so no one will think anything of you having it." He starts putting my jewelry into a nondescript black cloth bag. "And I have this for you," he hands me a small locket. It's got engraved writing on it. I can't read much but I know it says the equivalent of my name in Imperial. I open it. It's a small bit of black hair. I know that this is Dylan's hair that I had kept in a little box that was empty in the wardrobe. I had never told Seb about it though.

"How did you have this made so quickly? And how did you know that was our son's hair?" I ask.

"How did I not know? Who's lock of hair would it be if not Tema's? I wondered for a long time if you knew he was going. I never wanted to ask but since this is the last time, we might see each other, I want to know."

I shook my head, "No. I didn't know. Had I known I might have killed him and me. I thought he would be a pet. I only took the hair as a human custom." I looked up at him, holding the locket, "Thank you. And it says my name."

"I know you wanted some Imperial identification jewelry. This is close enough. I had it made a while ago I was just keeping it for a special time to give it to you. I guess now is that time. Keep it hidden until Earth joins the IGC, until then, as you know it's illegal for you to have."

I smile up at him wondering who he thinks I'm going to be meeting on Earth that would know what the Imperial written language looks like and even if they did they would probably only be an ex-pet like me. "I will."

He takes the locket and puts it around my neck. "And it's a reminder to you that Tema and I always existed and that you had this time with us."

Tears start running down my cheeks again and I'm on the verge of an ugly cry. "Maybe I should just take my chances and stay here. I could try to live on Fulior station."

He interrupts me, "No. It's not safe. I would worry all the time and it'd be no life for you. Stuck on a station confined to a room."

"No different than here," I admit. And then I almost think of something galaxy-shattering but before my mind can attach itself to the thought, Seb breaks my train of thought with his reply.

"No, it's different here because you are with me. Now prepare yourself. You must go soon. You're only allowed a small bag of nondescript items. Do you want to take your ball?"

I want to say 'no', but in actuality the ball and I have spent so much time together I can't leave without it. I take my rainbow ball from his hands without saying anything and set it on the bed next to the jewelry.

"Your clothing?" he asks moving to stand in front of the wardrobe again.

"Only the outfits that I chose."

"Not even the first outfits I bought for you?" he asks hurt.

"Okay," I feel guilty, "One of those too."

In no time at all, my little bag is packed. I could barely squeeze my ball in, but I really wasn't going to leave without it.

"Once Earth's government joins the UGC I will send some UCs to you and in time, depending how negotiations go, find you again."

"Okay," I say overwhelmed with all of this now. "And if there are no negotiations?"

"There will be," he says confidently.

"I want to take a video of you and our son. I'll hide it."

He shakes his head, "You know I can't allow you to do that." He touches the necklace over my clothing. You have Tema, my and your DNA in that lock of hair in the necklace and it has your name written in Imperial on it. It's enough. Anymore illegal things and they will find everything and take it from you." Seb pulls me into his embrace then. He runs his fingers through my hair but doesn't say anything else.

I give Seb all of my practical information in a rush of information, just in case he ever comes to Earth and wants to find me. I don't know how well Imperial technology works, so I tell him my full name and tell him the city and hemisphere I will be living on. He saves it all in Imperial on his computer. Then he closes it, stands and looks down at me.

"Seb," I try not to get too emotional; I want to be able to say 'goodbye'. "I'm so grateful to you that you bought me and took me on this journey." Then, I can hardly say the next sentence, "I'll miss you every day."

He takes me into a great embrace and kisses me. When he pulls away, he says, "Go with the gods, my Ensley."

An hour later, I walk off of his ship free, I'm no longer a pet. As I walk down the hallway towards the hatch that is connected to the passenger cruiser, all the Imperial men I have grown to like are there. They let me pass and as I walk by they all wish me, "Go with the grace of the goddess."

Tears well up in my eyes, this is something that you say to someone who you know you will never see again alive.

At the end of the line is Seb's squire. I can't help it, I give him a hug, "Thank you for everything. For teaching me Imperial for the extra food and most of all for your company when I wasn't the best company."

He shakes his head, "No Ensley. There's no thanks to give. You were never a pet. Go with the grace of the goddess."

Seb is behind me and puts a hand on my back as he leans forward and opens the hatch to the other ship. When it opens there are Imperial men waiting. Seb turns to me, "Go with the grace,"

I kiss him before he can finish. Then I memorize his surprised face and walk on to the Imperial cruiser smiling. I ended my relationship with Seb on my terms. In a human way and this allows me some closure on my time as a pet. I feel in some ways that I won this whole alien abduction thing, not without battle scars though.

. . .

ON THE IMPERIAL PASSENGER CRUISER, I am greeted by human women of every shape, size, and age. All going home. One thing I do notice as well is that no one has a child with them. We are all returning alone.

The mood on the Imperial Cruiser is somber and even though it is a passenger vessel, they have overfilled it, so not all of us have beds.

I don't have a bed but I don't care, it's only a seven-day journey, and there is food, people to talk to, and most importantly, we are returning to Earth as free women.

I've heard that some humans decided to stay on as free beings. That their masters were lucky enough to find occupations for their former pets. It makes me wonder what my future would have been if Seb had been a freighter captain instead of in the Imperial military. I look at my reflection in the window and touch the necklace he gave me, fantasizing that I could have been like his wife, and maybe we even could have had a family together.

However, as the days pass, I start thinking about what my future on Earth will be like.

I think about my family and friends.

I wonder if they stopped looking for me.

If they had had a funeral for me.

I feel terrible now, wishing that I was still with Seb. *He bought me and didn't want to return me*, I remind myself, but I can't bring myself to hate him. I still love him despite everything he did to me. But I keep telling myself that the best thing for me now is to return to Earth. I hope that thinking it all the time will help me to really believe it. I think I might need to get a tattoo that says, 'I belong on Earth.'

AFTER A WEEK OF TRAVEL, we slow as we enter the Solar System and start passing familiar landmarks, if you will. I think my heart is going to burst when I look out the window and see Jupiter. It's magnificent, and I almost cry, thinking, *I'm almost home.* I touch my necklace and think of Seb. I still miss him but seeing Jupiter has reminded me of my life before and has given me just a spark of inspiration to get my life back. It's the first time I have felt even the slightest bit of excitement about returning to Earth and living a healthy human life again.

When we finally reach Earth, the Imperial cruiser sends us down in stealth transports, so we will not be detected by inferior human technology. We are told that the IGC will be reaching out to our human government, none of the Imperial men can understand that we are not yet united under one government to discuss terms of membership. We are all advised not to say that we have been taken by members of the Empire as pets. They don't specifically mention any punishments if we do tell, but I think we all know enough about the Empire to know that we would probably just 'disappear' or have an unlucky accident if we tell the truth about where we have been.

I want more than anything, to be honest with my friends and family, but I know there's a good chance that no one will believe me anyway and I am afraid of the Empire, even if they are across the galaxy. And I want to be normal. I don't want to be a freak on a documentary about aliens, worried about the Empire trying to kill me, so unless this all becomes common knowledge, I'm just going to tell people I was abducted and held by traffickers or something. I haven't worked out the details yet.

When we exit the transport, I am hit by the humidity, heat and smell of earth. I almost laugh, realizing where we are. Now I understand why so many human pets were from South America, we have landed in what the women around me are saying is Peru. Apparently, it's the most commonplace for aliens and humans to rendezvous.

I've no idea how I'm going to get back to New York, but I'm glad to be back on Earth. I kneel on the moist ground and pick up the wet dirt in my hands and say out loud, "I never thought I'd see you again dear sweet dirty earth." I know tears are running down my cheeks, but I don't care. I'm overwhelmed by the smell of my home planet, and the other human women surrounding me all of us crying for joy.

AFTER WE HAVE all had our moment, we prepare to trek to the nearest village.

We must hike through the jungle, and I'm not looking forward to it. I have never been in a jungle and especially not at night. As we begin walking, with every stray plant that brushes my skin, I imagine it to be a snake or a spider coming to kill me. Every body of water we pass, I imagine alligators and piranha in it. My brain is on high alert, and I can't be sad or happy. I'm just in survival mode now trying to get to the village that some of the women promise is nearby. I keep telling myself, *This is all you have to do then you will get to an airport and go home. Focus on home.*

After two days in the jungle, we walk into the nearest village from where we had been dropped off by the Imperial transport. We must have been a strange sight to see walking into the small and rural village. Women of all different ages and colors wearing a mix of strange galactic clothing and covered in sweat and dirt, carrying strange belongings. A few of the women with us immediately bolt into the village and start screaming their 'hellos.' I don't speak Spanish, but I know 'Hello, I've returned!' when I hear it in any language.

The rest of us just stand stupidly in the middle of the muddy village. A light rain is misting everything, and I just close my eyes and enjoy it. I imagine that Mother Earth is washing me, no baptizing me clean of everything that I've suffered from in the galaxy. I've not felt the rain or mud or wind or plants since I was abducted, and my body now is being reunited with Earth, and it feels good. I think that even if I never leave Peru, as a human, I'm meant to live on Earth. This is my home, and I am human. Nothing else. I'm shocked that I could have felt any other way a couple weeks ago, that I would have wanted to stay somewhere that I didn't belong. But I don't have too much time to dwell on those thoughts as I'm pulled into the present.

One of the women who had run into the village is returning with villagers behind her. They carry colorful blankets and some food for us. I don't know what she's saying chattering on to us so excitedly and fast, but it's obvious she's inviting us back to her home. Her village surrounds us, and I don't remember the last time it felt so good to smell so many humans around me and to see so many human faces. And brown eyes. Imperial people only have green or grey. I can't help myself; I start to cry again. An old woman puts her arm around my waist, as she is so short, it won't extend around my shoulders and comforts me in her language. I just keep crying as we walk, and I am not alone.

A lot of women are crying; it's as if we can all relax now, and we can be human.

We enter a large house, there are chairs to sit in and the smell of bread in the air. A grey cat runs across my path, and I think *I won't miss the color grey for a long time.* Then it's time to take turns making phone calls. It's decided, I hear this from the 10-year-old boy as he is the only one who speaks some English, that the people who have been gone the least amount of time should use the phone first as they have the best chance of getting in touch with someone immediately. However, this plan is abandoned when none of us, I'm included in this group, know anyone's phone number. I need a computer or a smartphone, not an old-fashioned telephone. Thankfully, the 10-year-old boy has a tablet, and so we all take turns emailing our loved ones. I unfortunately cannot access my email. It's been too long since I used it and I need to verify my password with my mobile phone.

I'm crestfallen and feel frozen, not knowing what to do next. Another woman takes pity on me and without asking, calls the American Embassy for me from the phone number on the website. I'm the only American. The helpful woman hands the phone to me and I start crying when I hear an American on the other end of the line. I've not heard my own countrymen in years now. I breakdown in uncontrollable sobs. I can't speak. The American woman on the other end must be used to abductions, though, because she continues to talk to me. She reassures me that everything will be fine and that I'm going home. After a few minutes, I manage to pull myself together and find my voice to answer her. When I tell the Embassy woman my story, I decide to stick to the truth as much as possible.

I tell her that I was abducted and made to be a sex slave but in South America. I feel bad about saying, 'South America' as these Peruvian people have been nothing short of saviors for me, but I can't say aliens abducted me.

The next day we are all driven to the capital and dropped off at our various embassies. It all seems so bizarre. I've no passport and no money. I'm worried that because there's no record of me going to Peru that they won't believe me when I say who I am, but I decide to stick to the truth and tell them that I was abducted from Central Park. I'm forced to make a police report. I tell them that I can't really remember what the men who abducted me looked like. I only tell them that they all wore green clothing. And that my abductors had me blindfolded a lot of the time or kept in dark rooms. I also tell them that I didn't pick up any names as I don't speak Spanish.

The authorities look at me like I must be the dumbest American they have ever come across, not learning any Spanish after a few years in captivity and only hearing Spanish that entire time. But from my years of being a pet, I give them my best blank and stupid faces, and they believe I am really this dumb. In the end, no one is charged, and the US Embassy provides me with a room with a desk, no bed or anything, only somewhere to rest before they make me an emergency passport and put me on a plane back to New York.

By the time the plane takes off, I think I have been awake for days.

I'm so tired. When I arrive and walk through immigration, I feel like the luckiest person to be alive as if there should be dramatic music as I exit JFK airport. But there isn't and there is no one to greet me. I'm surrounded by humans, my people, but everyone is a stranger.

The embassy had given me a loan with interest of a couple thousand dollars, and so I grab a yellow cab to a cheap hotel I know, hoping they will have a room which they do.

The next day, I begin to rebuild my life. I start by getting a pay as you go phone.

Then I go to my parents' old home and try to find out where they have moved to. After a few phone calls, I find them. They are overjoyed when they hear the sound of my voice. They come and meet me and I move in with my parents while I start again.

. . .

171

TWO YEARS LATER, I'm looking out over the city at night from my balcony when I hear a noise in the kitchen. It sounds like an intruder, but I think that *It can't be. I live on the 46th floor of a nice building in Manhattan.* I still say, "Who's there? I've got a gun."

Then to my surprise, a little grey-skinned Imperial boy walks out. With my eyes. I recognize him immediately.

I drop my wine glass, not caring that it shatters all over the balcony and run to him.

The boy backs away, obviously not knowing me.

"Dylan," I say. "I'm your mother." I mentally switch on the translator I've not used in years, hoping it will still work so that I can at least understand his words. My heart is pounding, and I wonder for a minute if I'm dead, and this is heaven or the Imperial afterworld. I can't help but wonder if I jumped off the balcony to prove to Seb that I do have an Imperial soul after all.

Then I hear a familiar voice that I could never forget but that I haven't heard in years. I look up and see Seb who has walked out of the shadows and is standing behind Dylan. He looks the same as he always did with his uniform, and his long black braid down his back.

I feel like I might pass out.

"The boy doesn't' have the trans..."

He can't finish his sentence because at that moment I stand up, go to Seb and kiss him passionately. He's surprised, but after a second, kisses me back and takes me into his strong embrace.

When I come to my senses, I look back to Dylan, realizing all of this is real, and I'm not dead, "How are you here?" My heart is beating so quickly and this all seems so much like a dream I wonder if I'm having a heart attack or if my wine was poisoned.

"We had some time, and Tema wanted to see you," Seb says as if is the most natural thing in the world.

I look into his grey eyes, my eyes reflect back at me, "Tell him that not a day has gone by that I have not thought of him." I open the small silver locket I always wear around my neck and show him his hair inside.

Dylan touches the small piece of hair and then looks up at me and says, "Mother."

I begin to cry. I take him in my arms and hug him tightly. I smell his hair and think; *He still smells the same.* I close my eyes, remembering how much I loved being his mother when he was just a baby. "I thought I would never see you again. Either of you. I'm so happy you are here. But how is this possible? I still don't understand. I assume Earth rejected the IGC since we never heard anything about it. Are you here to take me back as your pet? Explain before I lose my mind," I demand of Seb still not letting go of Dylan.

Seb smiles, "I heard you calling for me from across the galaxy."

At first, I don't understand what he means, but then he holds up my book about my experiences with him onboard an Imperial starship and give him a sheepish smile. "I needed to do something to make money. I didn't want to sell any of the jewelry you gave me. I also wanted to tell my story, even if people thought it was only fiction. I wanted to find peace with what had happened between us. I also wanted to write about our son, so that I could still remember him as real, a name I could see on paper," I explain to Seb as I run my hand through Dylan's long black hair. "I wrote the book for me, for you both and all the other humans that were taken as pets."

Seb nods his understanding, "I thought the sections you wrote from my point of view were amusing, and just so we are clear, I would have never allowed the priest to touch you like that in the shrine."

"Okay so some parts were embellished," I admit. "What can I say? Sex is popular all over the galaxy."

"Indeed," he says. "And I've missed my little pet so much."

MY HUMAN PET EXPLAINED

"My Human Pet" is not meant to be just another science fiction romance to be taken at face value, and there are many deeper meanings to it. However, for many readers, these not-so-subtle points were missed, so I will briefly explain.

* * *

I begin the story with the words, "Shark attack," because it is more likely you will get eaten by a shark than abducted by aliens.

* * *

Ensley is proud to be a New Yorker because the press and propaganda in the US she has grown up with have told her she should be. The other women treat Ensley badly because she is from New York and because of the press and propaganda they have grown up with. If you hate Ensley for her behavior but can't see anything wrong with how the other women treat Ensley in that cage, you are just as prejudiced against anyone, not from the place you are from, as all those women are.

* * *

I purposely did not describe any characters' ethnicity until the aliens came in because I wanted to prove how prejudiced we all are based on where we are from in the first chapter. Once we know the women's ethnicities, it shouldn't change anything except to let readers know that Ensley is the smallest and the weakest.

* * *

As for language and readers saying, "Oh, how can the aliens be so advanced and not know Ensley is sentient?" Just like in the past on our own planet, there was propaganda that certain ethnicities were less cerebral than others. It was thought by Europeans until the 19th century that many ethnicities could not learn how to read or think complex thoughts. If you read to the end of "My Human Pet," you will realize that Seb figures out that everything he was told about humans is all government propaganda and that humans are no less intelligent than aliens (which is the whole point of the story, again and again, from chapter one and the women fighting because of where they are from to humans being seen as pets, it's all just propaganda from more important people than Seb or Ensley molding them into what their governments what them to be. It is the same with the women in the cage. The US has molded us into hating one another based on where we are from, the countryside or the city, the south, north, west coast, Midwest, etc.).

* * *

Half the sex in the book is not supposed to be romantic. It is sex for sex's sake. Primal, animalistic, and physical urges that have nothing to do with how one thinks. The sex in the book only becomes romantic after she and Seb get to know each other better. This was not a mistake.

* * *

When anyone is taken against their will, sold, and still remains a captive, no matter how "comfortable" the circumstances are, they are still slaves because they cannot make their own choices. What becomes confusing for Ensley is that she has fallen in love with her captor and is experiencing Stockholm Syndrome. This is why when she sees Jupiter, she asks how she ever could have doubted that she would want to return home.

* * *

If you don't think that Seb returning for her with their son is not a HEA or at least HFN, then I seriously question your understanding of relationships. Especially when Seb tells Ensley that he read her book (which is literally My Human Pet), it becomes clear readers don't know how much of what is written in this book is true because she says, "sex sells."

You, as the reader, must decide whether what Ensley told us was the truth or not.

* * *

If you could identify all of these themes, and understand the story, thank you, and well done. It was a book not just about aliens but about the human condition.

* * *

I will release my next book and put out a blog about the historical figure that inspired me for "Volunteer 4711." Some of you might already be able to guess from the blurb who it might be. "My Human Pet" was inspired by Ota Benga which I have a blog about if you are unfamiliar with his biography.

With best wishes,

Olympia
  xx

ABOUT THE AUTHOR

I write science fiction about humanity's relationships with aliens and artificial intelligence. To build my stories, I do not shy away from explicit encounters or highly emotional scenes. My books are not for the faint of heart but are observations about the human condition.

You can order her next book on Amazon:
    Volunteer 4711

Volunteer 4711

I was forced to volunteer.
Transported to an alien world.
Stolen by an alien pirate.
I must integrate to gain my freedom.

Printed in Great Britain
by Amazon

87621326R00109